SEEING OFF THE JOHNS

SEEING OFF THE JOHNS

^{BY} RENE S. PEREZ II

CINCO PUNTOS PRESS
• EL PASO, TEJAS •

FIRST EDITION
10 9 8 7 6 5 4 3 2 1

Library of Congress Cataloging-in-Publication Data

Perez, Rene S., 1984-
  Seeing off the Johns / by Rene S. Perez II. — First edition.
      pages cm
Summary: For Concepcion "Chon" Gonzales, the year that high school athletic stars John Robison and John Mijias left for college and never made it was the beginning of a new life in his small town and the first time he understood about love.

ISBN 978-1-941026-11-3 (hardback)
ISBN 978-1-941026-12-0 (paper)
ISBN 978-1-941026-13-7 (EBook)

  1. City and town life—Fiction. 2. Bildungsromans. I. Title.
PS3616.E74346S44 2015
    813'.6—dc23   2014032016

BOOK COVER AND DESIGN BY ZEKE PEÑA

For Hammonds and Mejares,
and for Natalie Rose

BEFORE

When word of the greatest tragedy in the history of Greenton made it back to town, the banner still floated over Main Street. "Hook 'em, Johns," it read. It had burnt orange Texas Longhorns printed on both sides, the iconic symbol of the university the Johns were speeding toward—the symbol they were to wear on their ball caps come spring. There had been a police escort and the shutting down of Greenton's businesses for a brief period so that its citizens could cheer on the young men all along the parade route—down through Main Street, under the banner, and out of town. After all, a Greentonite rarely made it to UT Austin, but for two of their own to enter its gates on baseball scholarships in one year warranted nothing less than a full-on celebration, a deep-seated compulsion to see off the Johns in style. They had graduated less than twenty-four hours before, walked across the stage set up at the Greenton High gymnasium, barely standing out from their classmates in their green caps and gowns. Now they were set to depart. By the end of the day, the Johns would be in Austin, unpacking in their new dorm, getting ready for summer classes and—most important—anticipating workouts the next day with their new coaches and teammates.

The fact that such a spectacle had been made of the Johns leaving town kept both the Robisons and the Mejias guarded and ill at ease in a time that should have been marked by unchecked emotions and copious nagging—"Are you sure you have the directions, have you checked the fluids in your car, the tire pressure?"

Arn Robison and his wife Angie left home in their Black Lincoln Town Car following John—their only child—as he made his way to John Mejia's in his 1993 Ford Explorer, all of his possessions in the world filling up half of the truck. In the Mejia's driveway, Robison got out and had a small conference with Mejia, one like the many they'd had throughout their high school careers: Mejia coming over to the mound from third base to give Robison his scouting report on a hitter from Falfurrias; Mejia behind the line of scrimmage stepping out from under center to turn and face his tailback Robison before returning to the business of calling his *Huts* and *Mississippis* and *Blue 42s*. Their in-game conferences were part of the legend of the Johns.

When they had their conference that morning—the morning of their leaving—presumably about how to put Mejia's belongings in Robison's truck—though it could have been about anything—people took photos. On-lookers exchanged stories and memories—their favorites from the Johns' greatest hits—as though any of them had a game or play to talk about that hadn't been witnessed by everyone else in town. The Johns broke their huddle of two quickly and set to loading the Explorer in under ten minutes—two large duffels, a trunk, a guitar, four plastic bags of non-perishables and four frozen meals in Tupperware that Mrs. Mejia made in the days leading up to the boys' exodus.

When the car was packed, there were perfunctory hugs and kisses. Later the Robisons and Mejias would come to remember the spectacle of that day with bitter regret. They had allowed themselves to be caught up in the hype, had condoned the hero-worship of two young men who were not yet done being boys in Greenton's frenzy and adulation. Under the prying gaze of their neighbors and peers, each boy had only allowed his parents a half hug and kiss before they got into the Explorer. They had, after all, reputations and images to maintain.

That day, the Mejias had to share their son with Araceli, the girlfriend he was leaving behind. She was still in high school, a senior. But they were used to sharing John with her. The kiss John Mejia gave Araceli, though, was as truncated and restrained as the affection he gave his parents. He leaned in close to whisper something to her, but she didn't seem as keen as Robison to have her interactions with him play out in the form of whispers and nods. She pulled away and—very clearly to the audience's eyes and ears—said, "Fine" and wiped her eyes.

The Johns got in Robison's Explorer. Their parents flanked the truck, two Mejias at the passenger door and two Robisons at the driver's. Tears were shed. Each parent leaned into the window that framed their son and, it seemed, tried to climb in to steal last minute hugs, egos be damned.

Then it was done. There was nothing more to say but goodbye. The parents stepped back from the truck in unison, like a space shuttle being shed of its rocket boosters. They stood on their respective sides of the Explorer, crying and beaming with pride and holding on to each other. Robison turned the engine.

The crowd outside the Mejia house fell silent. The police car waited expectantly at the curb. The Explorer pulled out of the drive and behind its escort. Robison stood on the brake so that he and Mejia could wave goodbye to their loved ones one more time. This having been done, the lead police car driver hit his siren. Everybody cheered, even the parents, having been pulled, half-heartedly, into the mob.

The police car took off, and the Johns followed. They got to the end of Sigrid, drove up Viggie to Main, and took that street out of town to the sounds of cheers and "The Eyes of Texas" blasted out over a P.A. system someone had set up for the forty seconds it took for the truck and its cargo of two to pass by, never to look back. But those forty seconds were worth it. No one could ever take those forty seconds away.

The crowds dispersed, talking of the season the Longhorns would surely have. Many were bold enough to forecast a trip to Rosenblatt Stadium in Omaha, a place some Horn fans called Disch-Falk North. Others were talking about their plans to go up to Austin to watch the Johns play at the park they themselves were already calling Greenton North. Finally they came back down to Earth, where there was work to be done and summers of mischief and sloth to be embarked on, smiling and with as much joy in their hearts as forty seconds can ever in a million years give to a whole town full of people.

SUMMER

Concepcion 'Chon' Gonzales didn't partake of Greenton's joy in those forty seconds. Instead he forced himself into eighty seconds of fake sleep interrupted by the sounds of sirens and the loud hootings of his neighbors and parents. Even his little brother Pito went out to cheer them on. The traitor. Chon pretended to sleep through the Johns' parade to prove some point—a point he couldn't quite define—to his family and to all of Greenton, but the town failed to notice his silent protest.

The night before, Pito made a big deal of asking their mother to wake him up early so that he could join in the morning festivities.

"Promise me, Mama," he had begged, unnecessarily.

Chon's parents wanted Pito to witness what could result from hard work and skill, but they knew about Chon's sulky dislike of John Mejia so they didn't say much.

"Alright. Go to bed," their mother said.

Pito clapped his hands excitedly and went to his room, avoiding his brother's eyes. In the silence that followed, the rock chords of a beer commercial blaring from the TV underscored Chon's anger at his brother and now at his parents. Chon sat at his end of the couch while his parents sat at the other, making a big deal of not mentioning the obvious—John Mejia's spectacular success.

Chon spared them any further awkwardness by getting up, grumbling something about being tired after last night's partying, and went to his room where he pretended to be asleep.

Chon hadn't always cringed at the thought of the Johns, particularly at the thought of Mejia. His animosity was only four years old. It had existed for just under a quarter of his life and for the entirety of what he considered to be his manhood, from thirteen to that very day.

In elementary school, Chon had been the cutest and—that indicator of alpha male status—the tallest boy in his grade. Even then, it was clear to him that he could have for his girlfriend any girl he chose. Naturally, he chose the prettiest girl in school. From third grade through seventh, Chon Gonzales, the boy with the glowing hazelnut/amber brown eyes, had Araceli Monsevais at his side.

During this time, Chon played on Little League baseball and football teams alternately with and against the Johns. At many of these games, Araceli would sit in the stands and cheer Chon on. While she was there, more accurately, to cheer on her cousin Henry, who seemed always to be on any team Chon was on, Chon played every second in right field as though she were there for him and him only. He would make to run in the direction of any ball that was hit. In the event a ball was hit his way and he missed it, as he was likely to do, he would hustle to pick it up, try his damnedest to throw it where it needed to go, and pray that Araceli couldn't see from the stands the tears that were burning in his eyes.

One of the lasting memories of Chon's baseball days was the game when he had the good luck to smack a high curve—one the too-young pitcher he was facing shouldn't have been throwing—with the sweet spot of his TPX, launching the ball into left-center field. After a sprint fueled by the desperation of a boy prematurely aware of the fleeting nature of Little League glory in a small town—a boy who knew that he wasn't likely to ever hit a baseball that well again—and with the benefit of a throwing error from a left fielder who had fought with his center fielder teammate for the ball, Chon had enough time for a stand-up triple. He slid—Pete Rose-style—anyway. It was a great experience while it lasted. It should have made a great memory, except that when he got up and dusted himself off, he realized that Araceli hadn't seen it. She had gone to get candy at the concession stand or to use the restroom or to do something that caused her to miss Chon's only hit of the day—and the only extra-base hit of his short career.

That was the story of their relationship: poor timing and an inability to recreate a moment of glory.

That night, on the eve of the Johns' departure from town, Chon lay awake thinking of possible ways in which he would win back the woman he felt destined to be his. Tomorrow Mejia would have the future and the rest of the world on the end of a string. With all of that good fortune coming to him, couldn't he leave something behind?

John Mejia haunted Chon's thoughts. But it was hard to extricate Greenton's Romeo from its Juliet, if even only mentally—Chon couldn't picture any version of Araceli without John Mejia at her side, at least any version he would want to focus on. The only John-less images he had of her were pre-John images.

The truth was, Chon could really remember hardly anything about his years with Araceli. How much attention did any boy pay to a girl before he is interested in sex? His interest in her was pure and fleeting, like so many other interests he picked up and put down when he was young. Sure they held hands, but only until their hands got sweaty. Sure they kissed, but what good is kissing when the kissers have no idea what it could lead to? They hadn't even started talking on the phone in earnest teenage obsession.

And that's all the Araceli that Chon could lay claim to: a pre-John one, an Araceli that Mejia seemed happy to concede to Chon, because he was never jealous.

Mejia never registered Chon as a threat to his relationship with the most beautiful of Greenton's daughters—not when he first took her from Chon, and not any time thereafter.

On the day he took her, a day at the beginning of seventh grade, Mejia made a big deal of waiting at Araceli's locker to walk her to class. That was something Chon had done every now and then with Araceli, the girl he called his girlfriend, but who hadn't called him her boyfriend in quite some time. While Araceli had achieved a firmness and amplitude of body in the summer between sixth and seventh grades, Chon, whose voice had not yet begun to break and squeak much less dip to the smooth baritone tenor of John Mejia's, hadn't seemed to notice. Once again, timing was off. Except that, this time, it was Araceli who hit for the fences and Chon who missed seeing it.

John Mejia didn't miss it though. Chon never stood a chance against so much facial hair and muscles and bass and testosterone and so much burgeoning local celebrity. The Johns were already beginning their athletic takeover of the hearts and minds of Greenton. Strained as his relationship had become with Araceli, Chon wouldn't have stood a chance against the opposition of any interested older boy. He didn't fault Araceli for having snubbed him for one of Greenton's two crowned princes. He simply figured, naively, that when his maturity and biology caught up to hers and to Mejia's, he would win her back.

Time didn't treat him so well though. He was plagued with such a case of acne that not even Christ would have touched him. He shot up in height from five nine to six four but couldn't seem to gain an ounce of weight. Come eighth grade, he was a freak of nature and Araceli was dating the freshman starting quarterback and third baseman of Greenton's most important varsity squads.

Chon lay in bed the morning of the Johns' departure without a clue. How would he get Araceli back? His complexion was finally clearing. He'd managed to put on eight pounds during his junior year of high school. He no longer only saw ugly when he looked in the mirror. After some late night misadventures with Ana at work, he knew that he was walking around with hot blood in his veins and some experience to complement the desire that emanated from between his legs, controlling his every thought sometimes. But still Chon could only think of Araceli's beauty in the context of her prom picture with Mejia.

So he slept uneasily, waking up from his light sleep when he heard Pito ask, "Did I miss it?" Their mother assured him that he hadn't and shushed him up.

Chon could have just rested there quietly, staring at the ceiling or at the TV on mute or reading a magazine. Instead he forced his eyes shut and crammed his head between his pillows. Sleeping through the town's final celebration of the Johns would harden Chon's resolve to continue loathing a guy who never really did him wrong.

The first rush of applause, when the Robison family drove by his house en route to the Mejia's, didn't make Chon open his eyes. And he had fallen asleep for real by the time the sound of sirens and shouts passed by him some time later, waking him for the second it took him to realize what was going on. He closed his eyes in a calm and sinister fashion, like he imagined a super villain would. Because isn't that what he was—Bizzaro trying to take Lois Lane from Superman?

When the day was over, he could tell himself he had slept through seeing off the Johns. He would emerge from his bomb shelter, guns in both hands, ready to fight the Nazis or the Russians or the Iraqis. He would right the wrong that had never really been done to him in the first place.

For good measure, and to put some distance between himself and his own stand—because what kind of stand would it have been if he'd backed down straightaway after not having made his point—Chon didn't leave his room or get out of bed until three pm, thirty minutes before he had to go into work. He slammed the door to his room behind him and took the quickest of showers, brushed his teeth, slapped on some deodorant, combed his hair, then hopped in his car, an '89 Dodge Dynasty that had been dubbed the Dodge-nasty by Chon's best friend in town and, thus, the known world, Henry Monsevais. Henry was also Chon's old Little League teammate and perennial bottom-of-the-order brother. And he was Araceli's cousin, younger by two weeks. Henry had taken the liberty of severing the cursive connection between the y and the n and scraping off the first two letters of the logo on the trunk of Chon's car. When Chon saw what Henry had done, he laughed and said, "It fits."

When, for the remainder of his sophomore year, everyone in school had taken to calling Chon "Dodge-nasty," he was less than pleased.

"I'm sorry, man. If I had known—" Henry apologized when John Robison said, "Later, Dodge-nasty" out the window of his Explorer as he cruised by. Chon cut Henry off.

"Don't worry about it," he said. He was at the pinnacle of teenage self-loathing. "It fits."

Everything looked normal on the way to work. There weren't any more or less cars on the road. The driver of every car loosened his grip on his steering wheel to pick up the index finger and pinky of his two o'clock hand in the form of a wave. There were more kids in the yards he drove by—playing football or hide and seek or whatever kids play—but today was the first Saturday of the summer, so that was to be expected.

When he pulled onto Main, he saw the "Hook 'em, Johns" banner bobbing up and down, lazing in its perch over town. It was almost enough to make Chon cringe except that the Longhorn symbols on either side of the banner reminded him that the Johns were moving away, on to bigger and better. They would meet new friends, new girls— women even—in Austin. Greenton, Texas and Araceli Monsevais and that microcosm of relevance—that blip that didn't even register on Mejia's radar—Chon 'Dodge-nasty' Gonzales were to be forgotten. They would be written off as a part of the quaint past.

"Good luck," Chon said, flipping off the banner, "and good riddance."

Chon parked the Dodge-nasty on the car-length path behind The Pachanga convenience store and gas station, worn bare to dirt by years of employee parking. Artie Alba, the store's owner who lived in San Antonio but kept close watch on his store through reports he would receive from his in-town cousins, had purchased the Greenton Filling Station and renamed it. He knocked out a portion of the wall behind the register to install a drive-through window for the convenience of drunks too lazy to get out of their cars to buy beer.

Someone had spilled soda on the floor in front of the fountain area. Judging by the stickiness of the syrup that remained, the soda had been spilled three hours before. The beer cooler was near empty which didn't make sense since beer sales were only permitted after noon, and the store's solitary unisex bathroom was a mess, bomb-shat diarrhea all over the bowl. This is what Chon could look forward to for half of the summer's work days, because now that he didn't have school as an impediment or an excuse, he would be splitting the mid-shift with Ana, which meant coming in after Rocha, the septuagenarian drunk with his Olmec complexion and his malformed hook of a baby-sized left hand and his refusal to do any of the work that he was otherwise able to do when The Pachanga was still the Greenton Filling Station and Art Alba still lived in town.

"It's my hand, bro," he used to say, when asked about the state of the store at the end of the 7 to 3:30 shift he worked exclusively. "Mi manito nanito."

Now all he would say if so confronted was, "Fuck you, kid. Do it yourself."

And so Chon would have to do just that: face lakes of high fructose corn stickiness, mountains of unstocked beverages in the tundra of the walk-in, and the aftermaths of shit-bomb tsunamis.

He walked to the back and put the mop bucket in the sink to fill before he even clocked in. He met Rocha at the wall-mounted time card tower. "How was it today?"

Rocha grumbled from the bottom of his throat, not bothering his tongue to syllablize nonsense.

"Well, the store looks really great."

"Chinga tu madre."

"¡Ay papí! I love it when you talk dirty to me!"

"Pinché maricón desgraciado."

His spirits lifted as they were, Chon mopped up the fountain area with a smile on his face. His day wouldn't turn shitty until he hit the bathroom.

After a few hours of cleaning and relaying between the cooler, the drive-up window (at the sound of the doorbell buzzer on the bottom window sill), and the counter (at the sound of the bells above the door) like Pavlov's dog, The Pachanga was clean, stocked, and operating as slowly as it did on any other day.

Chon had been sitting on the stool behind the register for as long as it took his mind to wander to thoughts of Araceli—which is to say it hadn't been long—when he was distracted by the honking of a car passing by. It took him away from his favorite image of Araceli, remembered from the previous year's luau-themed homecoming dance. She wore a bikini top—white with pastel polka dots of varied size, like stars approaching a spaceship Chon often fantasized he was piloting—with a simple flowerprint cloth tied at her waist and a pink lily in her hair. The Mejia goon in his blue board shorts, leather chanclas, and muscle-hugging designer tank top, though, was a part of that picture, a part Chon could only ever just blur out of focus, but never fully airbrush away.

He looked outside to see a line of cars making its way down Main to Viggie. It was a strange sight, so many cars on the road traveling in the same direction when there wasn't a baseball or football game to get to. Was there a funeral in town? No, the cars were going in the opposite direction of both the church and cemetery. Besides, how could someone in town have died without Chon hearing about it? No matter how good he was at shutting his eyes and separating himself from what went on around him, he would have heard that kind of news the second it hit town.

It wasn't just the cars. There were people on foot too, crying as they walked down the street. Chon felt like someone wading upstream in a rush of panicking hordes, unaware of the calamity and terror from which they were fleeing. His curiosity at the sight morphed to fear. That panic was interrupted by the bells over the storefront entrance. It was Henry, flushed and breathless.

"Holy shit, bro, they're dead," he blurted out. Henry's face was covered with sweat, much of which had collected at the corner of his mouth on his pathetic Fu Manchu whiskers.

"Who's dead?" Chon said.

"The Johns. There was an accident. They're dead."

Chon felt his eyebrow rise of its own volition.

"Give me the keys to the Dodge-nasty, man. Everyone's going to the Robison place," Henry said. He looked out impatiently at the cars and pedestrians making their way to the action. "Holy fuck," he said to himself.

Chon took his keys from his pocket and slid them on the counter. Henry picked them up.

"Alright, man. You're off at midnight, right?" He didn't wait for an answer. "I'll be back by then. Hay te watcho."

Then he left. After a short time, everyone seemed to have left . The streets of Greenton were empty, Chon Gonzales alone on his stool to contemplate what it all meant.

Andres and Julie Mejia had eaten breakfast and then made love. They'd planned on being louder, but it was as silent and meditative as the first time after their oldest son Gregorio was born. Goyo was asleep in his crib, put down after his changing and bottle. Andres would swear that the look in his eye that day had nothing to do with the fact that it was the day the doctor-mandated moratorium on sex had ended.

"I really didn't know," he said whenever Julie brought it up afterwards. It became one of their favorite stories to share in intimate moments. "And who says I would have waited one second longer anyway, no matter what any doctor said."

Andres had done some boxing in his teen years and some volunteer firefighting with the county. He had worked odd jobs stripping roofs and picking and hauling watermelons, at the same time serving as a mechanic's apprentice. All of this work led to his still impeccable physique, a source of pride and shame to Julie. She had always been big. On the arm of her Mexican Adonis, her Adanis, she figured all anyone could see was the disparity between the two of them. She couldn't see, like Andres did, like her sons did, like everyone did, that she wore every ounce of her weight perfectly—her face was exactly symmetrical save for a beauty mark above her lip on the right side, her hips and thighs would have broken the charcoal pencils of a thousand would-be artists trying to master curves, even her belly with its uniform softness which made Andres crazy when he wrapped his biceps and forearms around it—all of it transcended the oppression of Barbie, drove men who were into bigger women wild, and made men who weren't see how they might be.

When Andres and Julie were done, sweaty bodies glowing in the strange glow of daylight filtering in through the shades, they lay in bed thinking that life would be like this from now on. After a day at work—him at the shop, her at the library—it would be making love—fucking, if that was the case—at any time, volume, or place in the house they so chose. They were both thinking, though they didn't say so to each other, that they hadn't felt like this since they'd played hooky back in school—lied to mom about a stomachache or to dad about menstrual cramps. But now they had no one to lie to. There was no shame in being in bed in the morning like this, only pride. Pride in their boys and pride in themselves for having made them.

Julie got out of bed to shower. Then Andres did. Then they made love again, remembering their resolution to not stifle the moans and grunts and climactic screams that had been building up in them for twenty-three years. After this they took to the shower together, during which she scrubbed his chest and back and he massaged shampoo gently on her scalp. They stood dressing at their respective ends of the bed where their bureaus were. Andres made a playful lunge at her, and she laughed.

"No," she said. "We'll be late."

They took his truck, which he never took anywhere but to the shop or out on a call. He was not only Greenton's most trustworthy mechanic, he was its one-man roadside assistance. Goyo helped. Every now and then, John did too, as the case demanded it.

They hadn't even made it to the end of Sigrid when they were greeted by their neighbor Pedro Guerra who gave a shout to the couple and picked up his right hand, ring and middle fingers held down by his thumb.

"Hook 'em," he shouted, and flashed a two-tooth smile.

Andres managed to wait until he pulled onto Viggie before he burst into laughter. Julie couldn't hold it that long. Three other cars honked at the Mejias, extending the same greeting. They even saw other people salute friends and neighbors with their index fingers and pinkies. It seemed that the whole of Greenton was going to do this for the next four years, bathed in a sea of burnt orange until the boys graduated and went pro, as was their plan, and a new color was adopted. But pro ball teams didn't have hand signs like the Longhorns did. Hook 'em just might turn into Greenton's new hello.

Arn Robison had the fire going, coals nice and grey, grill warmed and ready for whatever flesh needed cooking. Andres and Julie walked straight to the Robison backyard to hug Arn and Angie. She was still as beautiful as she was when she met Arn. That made the couple a funny sight because Arn had lost most of his hair and gained quite a bit of weight in the interceding years.

The Mejias were always told not to bring anything but appetites to the Robison house. After so many dinners with them, they were finally comfortable in complying with the familiar directive. A fruit tray had been set out. When the Mejias arrived, Angie ran inside and returned with a tray holding four big New York strips.

"This is too much," Julie said, as she often did at the Robison's get-togethers.

"Who can begrudge us an indulgence on such a great day?" Arn looked up. But he was not talking about the weather, which was prefect by Greenton standards, the dry heat not so bad under the shade of a tree or, as in the Robison's case, a deck covering. Andres looked at Julie and they smiled their secret at each other. No one could.

"And in that spirit," Arn said, "a toast."

He held out a glass of bourbon to Andres while Angie poured a couple of margaritas in stemware waiting on the table. They raised their glasses, the four of them, and looked at each other as though they'd all just rolled out of bed after an afternoon of intimacy.

"To our boys," Angie said.

"To our Johns," Julie added.

"To our Johns," they all said.

They had always gotten on this well, despite their difference in age. The Robisons had their John late in life, after having been told they never would. Though the Mejias were in their early forties and the Robisons were well into their sixties, they were friends because their boys were friends, best friends. Well before Araceli sat down to dinner with the Mejias, they'd had John Robison over as a guest at countless dinners. They were not special dinners. The Mejias rarely strayed from their standard foods— fideo and meat, tacos and chalupas, easy ricotta-free lasagna, beef and, more rarely, chicken enchiladas. But they didn't have to be special. They were not about anything more than two friends hanging together outside of school, the diamond and the huddle.

The Robisons, on their part, seemed to regard the Mejias—as some people do with their friends who are more than two decades their junior—as younger siblings and as children of their own. The Mejias had felt a sting of embarrassment when they went to the first of their dinners with the Robisons. They knew the Robisons were well off—Arn was the youngest grandchild and sole remaining Greentonite of Samuel and Wilhelmina Robison, who'd made a small fortune on a ranch outside of town. Arn had inherited money from them. He'd worked hard all his life as a horse doctor and hit big on some investments. But the Mejias weren't prepared for the kind of food the Robisons were used to.

That first meal together, the Robisons served blackened catfish, which Julie thought was too fancy for her taste. Over a decade of dinners, though, the Mejias accepted that there would be the occasional lobster tail or swordfish or prime rib or hundred-dollar bottle of bourbon.

On that night—the night after the Johns headed to Austin—Arn grilled the steaks and served twice-baked potatoes he'd made earlier and left warming in the oven. The men switched to beers, the women to margaritas, with an occasional shot of the hard stuff in between. Angie brought out a stereo and CDs and looked for whatever stations could be caught from Corpus and Laredo playing the country and conjunto music that they all knew and loved, even Arn. The sun was flirting with the horizon, day with night, when the phone rang.

"They're probably already there," Angie said before she got up from the table. She didn't want John's first call home to go unanswered so she made to run to get it but slowed her pace when the tequila and bourbon hit her. She left Arn and the Mejias waiting at the table, their talk quieted in the hope that they could soon talk to their sons who were on the other end of the line.

Then they heard Angie scream.

On the stereo, George Strait sang that he would be in Amarillo by morning.

Chon's first thought—right after Henry brought him the news, picked up the car keys and ran around the side of The Pachanga to get in the Dodge-nasty—was that the Johns death was an act of God, given to him as a personal blessing because he was a good Catholic boy who had completed all of his sacraments and said grace before every meal. He was too ashamed to ever share that thought with anyone though, not with Henry or his mother or even Araceli if she ever asked. He would never tell a soul.

The thought died quickly anyway, almost as soon as it had come to him. It was replaced with the image of an old couple crying over the loss of their only son; of the mechanic who had brought the Dodge-nasty back to life after Chon had bought it for $350 off the street and his wife who had checked out books to him—Dr. Seuss to Mark Twain—weeping at the passing of their youngest. And of Araceli Monsevais, Goddess of Greenton and queen of Chon's dreams and imagination, crying. He thought of the lake of tears the people of Greenton were crying at that moment and was shocked. And shamed even further when he didn't feel the warm stuff on his own face.

He sat at the register in silence. Through the store's windows, he looked at a Greenton that was emptier, deader than he had ever experienced it before. He thought of the last time he'd seen the Johns. Araceli was sitting across Mejia's lap on the tailgate of his father's truck. Robison was sitting at the other end of the tailgate, entertaining a group of girls. The girls claimed to be friends, but were strategically elbowing each other away from the single John with malicious words told out of smiling mouths. They hungered for their sisters' blood and the bragging rights that being with Robison on graduation night, the very weekend he was set to leave town, would have afforded them.

There was a huge circle of cars around the fire pit at the Saenz ranch that night, all of them driven there by high school students who had known the Johns as classmates and teammates and all of whom would be embraced and regarded as old friends if they ran into them on some city street in the surely glorious future. That said, the Johns were left alone—not necessarily placed in the limelight, but looked at enviously from a distance as they always had been at Greenton High and in town.

Chon and Henry were walking from a trip to the keg trough when Chon was summoned.

"Hey Dodge-nasty," Robison shouted from his Chevy throne.

Chon looked at Henry. Henry shrugged. Chon made his way over to the truck.

"You really pulled through with the beer," Robison said, raising his plastic cup.

Chon had gone against his better judgment in providing access to the night's spirits. Though he didn't have a problem selling beer to minors, he had never sold anyone underage so much—three kegs that had gone skunky from having been dropped, rolled, and kicked from one end of the Pachanga's walk-in to the other. Chon knew that he could be fired, even arrested, if anything bad happened as a result of the beer he'd sold. He knew that every time he sold a six-pack to his contemporaries for ten dollars and kept the change.

"Didn't Jesus say, 'Drink up, folks,'—or something like that—at a wedding? So, you know, it was the Christian thing to do," Chon said, looking over at Araceli.

"Hi Chon," she said, with a little wave of her fingers. Mejia gave him a nod. This was why Chon had sold the kegs, this very exchange here.

"Yeah, man. Jesus. You're a pretty weird guy, you know that, Dodge-nasty?" Robison said. He was drunk.

"You know what, Robe? This is the first time someone's ever told me that when it didn't sound like they were trying to be mean," Chon answered back, trying his best to stare Araceli down, but out of the corner of his eyes.

"Hot damn, Dodge-nasty. You know how to make a guy feel good about himself," Robison shouted. His crowd of girls all roared with laughter.

"Hot damn, Robe, that's what I'm trying to tell you."

Robison gave Chon a pound on the shoulder.

"Alright, well, good luck in Austin," Chon said.

"Yes sir. And good luck to you here in Greenton," Robison said, not intending to be ironic.

Chon's eyes drifted past Araceli's in a deliberate show that took all of the will power he had. They met John Mejia's.

Standing there, face-to-face with his nemesis, Chon worked to convince himself that he and Mejia weren't too different from each other. Mejia wasn't better looking—at least not by leaps and bounds—than Chon. He had an athlete's build, sure, but a lean teenage baseball player's. All that separated them was a God-given and determinedly honed skill on the diamond—that and a future at a university in a city Chon couldn't even picture in his head outside of images of clock towers and capitol buildings he'd seen in books. And a present with the only person worth wanting in a one-stoplight town built on cattle and railroads and killed by bypasses and super-ranches.

"Good luck," Chon said.

Mejia gave him a nod and took a drink of his beer. As Chon walked away, Mejia told Araceli something that made her laugh. A fire burned inside Chon that made him wish things he would come to regret in a few short days.

The clock read 12:13 when Henry got back to The Pachanga. Chon was sitting in the dark in front of the store, unable to lock up because he'd given his keys to his best friend.

"You're late," he said when Henry got out of the car. He took the keys and caught a whiff of Henry. "And you're drunk. Where've you been?"

"Flojo's, man. Half the town is there, the other half is at church," Henry said opening the passenger door to the Dodge-nasty. He let his body fall into the car, ass-first.

"You mean you were drinking at Flojo's?" he asked Henry when he got in the car.

"Yeah man, they were letting anyone in. The sheriff was even there getting pedo. We had all posted up at the Robison place, the whole town. Then Goyo Mejia got there to be with his parents. I mean, you think everyone was wrecked before... When he got there, his mom came out to the porch to meet him and she, like, fell into his arms. That totally tore everyone up. He just stood there with her crying on him for so long he had to crouch down under her weight. His dad had to come out and help her up and into the house."

They sat there in the parking lot of The Pachanga, the car not turned on, Henry's story fogging up the car's windows.

"After about an hour, Goyo came out and asked everyone to leave. He said that his parents and the Robisons were going through a rough time and had asked if we could leave them alone to 'hurt over their sons.' He said it like that. He wasn't even crying, man. His face hadn't seen a tear all day.

"By that time the whole sidewalk in front of the house was covered in candles. Man, I can't even think of how so many candles got there so fast. That stretch of Viggie doesn't have a streetlight, you know? The whole street was lit with candles. The sidewalk was covered in front of their place, so they just kept putting them in front of other houses. They almost reach to your house. Anyway, everyone left. No one said where they were going, but half ended up at Flojo's and the other half at the church."

Chon waited for Henry to tell him more. But Henry was done. He just sat there, his hands over his eyes, breath coming heavily out of his nostrils. Chon turned the car on and drove him home.

He took Mesquite from Henry's house, a street that, along with Sigrid, served as the east end of Greenton's east-west bookends. A few blocks from Viggie, Chon could see the town's church strangely active. Half of Greenton must have been there, looking up at the cross with their hands clasped in prayer (like a button that has to be held down on a walkie-talkie for any correspondence to be transmitted), asking God, asking the beaten-bloody Jew on the cross—asking them both at the same time—why?

He went back over to Main Street. There was a truck pulled onto the sidewalk—like its driver had tried to park perpendicular to it and then drove right on ahead. Chon might have assumed this was one of the Flojo's loaded congregants if he hadn't seen someone, presumably the truck's owner, standing on the roof of the cab. Chon slammed the brakes, backed into a two-point turn, and drove toward whoever was caving in the roof of his truck.

He put the Dodge-nasty in park, rolled down his window, and was about to shout the man down when he saw it was Goyo Mejia, indeed drunk, clinging to the telephone pole he was parked next to, tiptoeing up, just inches below the bottom right quadrant of the banner that had been hung for his little brother and his little brother's best friend.

"Hey," was all Chon managed to say. The first half of the H was loud enough to be heard, but he let the *e* and the *y* die in a downward glissandoing diminuendo, like a trombonist running out of breath and letting his instrument's slide slip from his hand down to the ground.

Goyo was trying to stretch himself up the pole. Chon got out of his car to make his presence known, hoping that might make a difference. The danger of the situation had Chon standing on his toes, every muscle in his legs tense. When Goyo's balance would tip this way or that Chon would give a start in that direction, like he did at so many routine grounders in his Little League days, with about the same, if not less, efficacy.

Suddenly Goyo gave a shout of frustration and punched at the telephone pole, which had years of nails and staples in it announcing so many yard sales and church Jamaicas and lost pets. Then he gave another shout, this one out of pain. He fell to his knee, still on the truck's roof, and clutched at his bloody fist. Chon watched Goyo shift his focus from fist to banner, back to fist, then back again. Then he let go of his hand, laid both hands palm-side down on the roof of the truck, righted his stance, touched down and gave a leap.

Chon watched in awe. It was far more graceful a leap than Chon could have ever executed, drunk or otherwise. Goyo seemed to float in air, ascending inch by inch toward the night sky. He caught onto the banner, but it was secured to the poles so well that when the right side came down, the left still held. That changed what would have been an up/down trajectory for Goyo to an outward pull like Tarzan swinging on a vine and bought him in a belly flop onto the bed of his truck. A less determined, less inebriated man would have let go of the banner. But Goyo Mejia, clinging to a relic of his brother's life that might otherwise have been taken by another person, held on with his bloody hand.

Half of the banner ended up in the bed of the truck with Goyo. The other half was splayed across Main Street. Chon heard a madman's laughter, replaced quickly by the loud sobs of a person who had either broken his ribs or lost his brother. Probably both. But Goyo couldn't have been hurt too badly because he began reeling what was left of the banner into the truck. Chon got in his car then and left, hoping that Goyo wouldn't remember that he'd had an audience, that someone had seen him at his whisky-soaked, grief-stricken worst.

The house was empty when Chon arrived. Just like Henry said, candles lit his way home. In the time it took Chon to drop his friend off and bear witness to Goyo Mejia's freefall, the candles had crossed his front yard and were making their way to Sigrid, if not all the way to Laredo and Mexico beyond. Chon got in the shower wondering if his parents and brother were among the half of town praying to a cross or the other half praying to the bottom of a glass.

He lay down in bed thinking, as he always did—but in a totally different way—of

Araceli. He tried to imagine how she was hurting. He thought of how he would feel if she died, but he knew that it wasn't the same thing. His obsession with her wasn't the same thing as what she shared with John. He tried to think how he would feel if he lost his parents or his brother, but knew, without really knowing, that this wasn't the same thing as losing someone you choose to love who chooses to love you back.

Then he gave up trying her hurt on for size. He knew she was hurting, and that was enough. He wished he could tear open her being and kiss her soul in ways sweeter and more loving than he had previously wished he could kiss her mouth or her breasts or her anything and her everything. He said a small prayer of his own for the Johns and their families.

He fell asleep that night having solved the riddle of nearly every sleepless night before then: he thought of Araceli without John Mejia muddying the picture. All he had to do, it turns out, was to think of her for her own sake—without thrusting upon her the weight of his desires and expectations—to see her as someone who could need and hurt and want and lose just like he could.

Two days later, the memorial service had to be moved from the Greenton Funeral Home to the school gym to accommodate the expected turnout. Coach Gallegos, the man the Johns had taken to regional tournaments in football and a state tournament in baseball, said a few words about the heart the Johns displayed on the field of play. Mrs. Salinas spoke about a Mejia most of them didn't know, about the poetry he wrote and how he helped tutor his best friend and had sworn to do so through a tough academic life. "They had been thinking about academics at UT!" she said emphatically.

Dan McReynolds, who did the weekly football season addendum to the ten o'clock news—"The Friday Night Blitz"—drove in from Corpus and was the keynote speaker of sorts. He had been a fan of the Johns' style since he first ran highlights of them during their freshman year. It was through this show that the boys had become regional celebrities, especially when McReynolds began running tape of the boys' famous conferences at the line of scrimmage. He even began covering the Greyhounds baseball team during the spring, not just during the playoffs as was usually the case for AA teams from a town that made up so small a portion of KIII's viewership. It all paid off when he was in Austin to cover the state playoffs during the Johns' junior year. Greenton and AAAAA Corpus Christi Moody both lost in their respective semis. He did an exclusive interview with the boys that weekend and another when he came to Greenton to cover their signing with UT a few months prior to their deaths. During that interview, they made no show of lining up three different college caps and selecting one, as was the custom for such signings. In fact, they wore burnt orange for the occasion.

He talked about the young men he'd had the pleasure and good fortune of meeting. He'd become friends with them. He said that he had planned to cover them through college and the pros, sports or not, for the rest of his career. He gave a speech with as many sports analogies as he could fit in—he said the boys were running an option each with hands on the ball, each blocking for the other. He said that heaven was the end zone. He said that now they were in the stands cheering the rest of us on.

Chon listened and clapped along with everyone else. He had arrived early for the service, but already the gym was standing room only. He stood in back and, tall as he was, could not see the front rows of the service, where he assumed Araceli would be.

Throughout the service, the somber tone of the proceedings was disturbed by the sound of hyena-cackle laughing. People in the back of the gym where Chon was were exchanging confused looks and shaking their heads in disapproval. Single file lines

36

formed on either side of the gym, leading up to where the Robisons and Mejias sat. When Chon got close to the front, he could see that the strange high-pitched sound wasn't laughter, but Julie Mejia's wails of grief.

Chon was glad to see that there were not two closed caskets at the front of the gym when he got there. They had been left at the funeral home. There were only three very large pictures—one of each John's yearbook photos at either end of the stage and one of them when they had beaten Pleasanton to earn a trip to State their junior year. They each had an arm around the other. With their free hands they held up #1s.

Arn Robison and Andres Mejia were making an effort to shake the hand of every mourner who—out of respect or macabre curiosity—had taken a place in line to give their condolences. Angie Robison gave nods to people she knew and hugs to people she cared about and ignored the rest. Julie Mejia just cackled, clutching the arm of the son who was still with her. Goyo sat in a black suit and sunglasses, wiping his mother's tears and caressing her face with his swollen right hand. Patchwork sutures on his fist stuck out ever so slightly, like tiny shoelaces that needed to be tied.

Chon shook both fathers' hands, telling them he was so sorry. He had come from audience left, meaning he met Arn Robison first. When he got to Andres Mejia, he saw the Monsevais family sitting behind the Mejias. Henry was with his father, there to comfort his uncle and aunt who acted as though they'd lost one of their own because, really, they had. Conspicuously—and to Chon's great disappointment—Araceli wasn't there.

Sympathetic though he was to the families of the deceased, it was going to take more than a tragedy to quench his obsession. He still wanted to comfort Araceli, to make her feel better. He was removed from the initial shock of the Johns' death, from the reality of life's fragility and preciousness and whatever. His mind had wandered to more familiar selfish territory. He wanted to comfort her. He wanted to make her feel better. He wanted to save the day, to be her Band-Aid, her hero, to fill the roughly John-sized, boyfriend-sized void left in her heart.

He was tired from having closed the store the night before and having had to open up at five that morning because Rocha called in sick and Ana didn't answer her phone when Art called to ask her to cover. There was a bottleneck leaving the student lot. It was only 1:30 in the afternoon though. Chon would have time to go home, shower, and get to work on time. But he wouldn't get any sleep before going in to work.

He went to the funeral the next day with his family, even though he'd heard from Henry that Araceli wouldn't be there either. It was as well-attended as the memorial service. People stood in the wings, vestibule, and stairs leading to the church. The Gonzales family arrived an hour and a half early, affording them a small stretch of the pew in the farthest back corner of the church. They watched two caskets carried into church, an experience Chon hadn't expected to affect him as it did—he became lightheaded and would have fallen down if he weren't already sitting. They heard Father Tom's sermon and a Gospel reading, punctuated by Julie Mejia's crazy crying. Then the caskets were carried back out and loaded into hearses. The mourners got into their cars and followed the procession through town to the Greenton cemetery. Not Chon, though. He turned the Dodge-nasty left when all of the other cars turned right. He had come to church, having dressed in a shirt and tie for the second day in a row, and paid his respects to the Johns without any hope in the world of seeing Araceli. This gesture was enough to convince Chon, as he was sure it convinced his family and would convince Araceli if it came up, that his sympathy was sincere. He'd done his politicking and point proving. He didn't need to see a couple of mahogany boxes lowered into the ground.

John Robison's Explorer blew a tire and rolled over when he took a curve too fast just outside of Beeville, TX. Why the boys ended up there was anyone's guess. The quickest route to Austin from Greenton was to take 16 to San Antonio and 35 from there to Austin. It would have been a four-hour drive. As it was, they had either veered from that route after Benavides, going east to Highway 77 outside of Kingsville and taking that north. Or driven over to Corpus and taken the Harbor Bridge into Portland and up north. Whichever was the case, the Johns ended up on Highway 181. They filled the Explorer up in Papalote, which made the rollover crash they would get in some seventeen miles up the road that much more volatile. It was the cause of the Johns' caskets being closed. Lawyers were already, just three days later, making their way to Greenton from Florida and from all over Texas too, where class-action lawsuits were being organized against Ford and Firestone. Ambulance chasers hoped they could talk either the Robisons or the Mejias into foregoing the potential years-long wait of such a suit and make quick money in a settlement.

Representatives from both Ford and Firestone were at the funeral, where it was assumed they were sympathetic mourners from somewhere in South Texas. When a Firestone business card was revealed, a sheriffs's deputy unholstered his truncheon and an old man grabbed the hunting rifle that had been stowed in his truck. Neither said anything. They just held their weapons across their chests. The Firestone suits never even got to speak with the parents of either boy before they got in their cars and drove away, followed quickly by the Ford representatives who saw just how their presence would have been received had they had the chance to say who they were.

When Chon got to work, Ana was outside sitting on the ice machine, an old double-doored cooler, smoking a cigarette and hugging herself. The cooler was five feet tall, taller than Ana herself. She would hoist herself up onto it by way of a milk carton and a trashcan. The impression Ana's ass left on the top of the cooler would deceive anyone looking at it—granted that they knew what it was—into thinking it belonged to someone sexy. It didn't. Four foot, ten-inch tall Ana had a round, flat rump that was just like her breasts—big, maybe even at one time desirable. But time and gravity had caused them to wrinkle and grow flabby. Her legs, by comparison, were small, made so by a drunk driver who hit her when she was eleven. The accident left her looking like a dreidel, the block of her upper body carried around on the legs of a preteen girl.

"She's whoring herself now," Ana said, smoke coming out of her mouth with every word. "I mean, it makes sense. She has to do something to live." She shook her head, looked across the street at San Antonio in her mind, and emptied the rest of the smoke from her lungs.

"I mean, fuck. You know? Worst mistake of my life." She chain-lit a new cigarette, then stubbed out the old one on the cooler.

"Yeah," Chon said. She had sent her daughter Tina away to live with the girl's father in San Antonio because Tina had been caught smoking pot in the school parking lot with Charlie Marquez, who folks in Greenton called el camerón. The nickname, 'the shrimp,' was a derivation of the word jailbait, given to the man by his friends when he was in his twenties—when he still had friends who would claim him—because of his tendency to go after younger girls. Twenty turned to thirty and el camerón lost friends because he was rumored to still be chasing underage tail. Then he turned forty-three and got caught getting a blowjob from a fifteen-year-old (Tina) in the high school parking lot. Charlie was run out of town when the charges didn't stick because the kid who caught him, a hall monitor narc with a clipboard—who was sent out to the parking lot to find truants with cigarettes and vodka in Sprite bottles—was naturally traumatized by the sight of the black and white belly hair that led down to his junk. She couldn't say for sure that she saw Charlie's joint in Tina Guerra's mouth, but nonetheless Charlie was run out and Tina was sent to her father.

In the year since Tina left for San Antonio, she had been kicked out of regular school and sent to a juvenile disciplinary school, where she made contacts with would-be dealers and pimps, developed a pretty bad addiction to drugs—pills and coke when they were available, but crack and meth mostly—done a short stint in rehab, and attended outpatient counseling which was working until her father lost his job and insurance. Bexar county's LCDCs were less like counselors and more like probation officers looking to send an offender back into the system where they belonged. Most recently, she had run away and been involved in a string of home invasions with a guy named Terry who was wanted on three drug charges and a failure to appear. Over the past year, Ana had filled Chon in on the news of her daughter's troubles as they were reported to her from San Antonio. Each time, she ended her report, in reference to sending Tina to her father, by saying, "Worst mistake of my life."

Each time, Chon agreed with that statement—but in reference to something else.

A while back, Chon had talked a cigarette distributor into giving him a pack of his most expensive cigarettes. He thought he'd give them to Ana who always only smoked the cheapest cigarettes—Best Value, Skydancer, Leggett's—and would only splurge the extra buck or so on Camels every third or fourth payday. When Ana came in to pick up her paycheck, he handed her the green box of Nat Shermans. She stared at them for a minute. Then she said she didn't smoke menthols. She immediately shook her head, crossing herself.

"I mean, that was really nice of you," she said. "You didn't have to get these for me." Chon was confused—weird how moved she was by a pack of cigarettes he'd gotten for free. "I mean, not cause they're menthols. I just...Fuck—" She went to the back of the store, leaving the smokes on the counter. Chon was closing, the lights were off and the shop was locked up. Ana came to the front of the store, grabbed Chon, and began kissing him all over. He pulled back to look at her and ask what she was doing. When he did, he saw something in her eyes that had not been there before in all of the sexual encounters they had at her empty, cigarette-stinking house—he had stopped counting how many when it became something less than thrilling and more like embarrassing. What Chon saw in Ana's eyes was something like gratitude or an actual desire to be doing what she was doing with the person in front of her. She looked at him, kissed him on the head, then opened his pants and put him in her mouth.

Reeling from pleasure, Chon fell back onto the stool behind him. He looked out at Main Street through the store's windows, foolishly afraid that anyone would see what was going on. Ana relented for a bit, looking up at Chon with those new eyes, and scared him more than the thought of being caught with his pants down. Stroking him, she smiled and with a knowing shake of her head said, "You're so fucking wonderful, do you know that? If you were twenty years older, we'd never do this. You're too good for me. I'll never deserve someone like you, but thanks for being here now."

She went back to her business of thanking Chon. He looked down at this woman—forty-three years old, widowed once, with a delinquent daughter and two ex-husbands—working him vigorously, expertly, he thought, in her mouth. He was aware for the first time that she was more than someone with whom he was complicit in the act of using and being used. She liked him. The responsibility of that realization nauseated Chon. Because, while he was currently placed precariously between her teeth, he was not the only one in this arrangement who was made vulnerable in the frame of the floor to ceiling windows at The Pachanga's storefront

She had offered him a cigarette that night. He accepted it to avoid any conversation in the darkness outside of The Pachanga—Ana smiling in the moonlight like a gargoyle atop the ice machine, Chon still feeling aftershock tremors of pleasure running through his belly. When she lit a second and offered Chon another, he declined and drove home. Fancy as it was supposed to be, the cigarette tasted off to Chon.

"So Bill called you and let you know?" Chon asked. To Chon's mind, Bill Guerra wasn't such a bad guy—just a parent, like Ana, who couldn't deal with his lost-cause daughter. He wouldn't tell Ana that though.

"Fuck that asshole. He isn't telling me anything. The detective in her case has been calling me. They might bring him up on charges for letting her get into all this shit. It'd serve him right." Ana looked at her cigarette, which she'd lit crookedly. She licked her index finger and ran it up the side of her smoke to quell its diagonally advancing cherry.

"And you? Any news on your chula?" she asked.

"Yeah," Chon said, "her parents sent her to stay with some family friends over in Corpus. They didn't want her to be around all this craziness. They're going to keep her over there until school starts."

"Well, that sucks for you, Chon-chon. You wait for an opportunity like this to come along and your girl leaves the county." She laughed smoke through her nose.

"Ana, those guys died," Chon said, shaking his head.

"And? Death is a perfect opportunity for new love. That's how Bill got me—when Jo-Jo had his embolism. Believe me, in this life you get left so much that it doesn't matter how—if they die or leave you for someone else or even go gay or something like that. All that matters is if you get found by someone else. You know?"

So much of this struck Chon as wrong. But he didn't want to argue with Ana however much he hoped it wasn't true. He had lately realized that he could—if he chose to—change any of her beliefs or ideas by simply disagreeing with them. For that reason, he stopped disagreeing with her completely. He knew Ana was lost right now, had been for as long as he had known her. He resisted, as strongly as he could, her attempts at finding herself in him. They hadn't had sex in weeks.

"Anyway," Ana said in the wake of Chon's silence. She slipped off of the ice machine onto the trashcan and stepped down onto the milk crate. "Her parents are right to get her away from this place. It's like people around here aren't happy enough sharing the same however many square feet of town, they have to share their sadness over two boys most of them didn't even know."

Chon nodded, holding the door open for Ana. He went behind the counter and opened the register.

"You left me two tens," he looked at Ana.

"Just drop some from the safe," she said on her way to the back.

"Ana," Chon said when she came back with her purse on her shoulder, "they come once a week to fill the safe. We'll run out of tens if we drop them so many times."

It was Sunday. Rocha was off, so Ana had worked the first shift.

"Sorry, Chon-Chon, I promise I'll be a good girl from now on and be real careful with the register," she said, walking out.

"Ana," he called to her, "have you even closed your till?"

She stood in the doorway and stared at him. "No. Will you count it for me?"

"You know, you're a cashier. You have to count every now and then," he said, opening the drawer and counting the money in it.

"Not to close my till, not when you're here to do it for me," she said with a smile.

He looked up at her and rolled his eyes. A girl no older than thirteen walked into the store. She wasn't from Greenton, but Chon thought he recognized her. Ana walked to the counter, putting her purse down to wait for Chon to run her numbers in the register.

The girl interrupted Chon's counting. "Do you guys sell the stars?" she asked. "The John stars?"

"Yeah," Chon said, starting over on the dimes.

"How much are they?" the girl asked.

"$2.70...$2.80...$2.90..." He raised his index finger to indicate to the girl that he needed one minute. He wrote down the total.

"$5 a pop," he told the girl.

"Okay," she said. "I'll take five."

"Alright," he said. "That'll be $25. Just hang on a second. I have to open this register."

There were only seven nickels in the register. Chon looked at Ana and at the nickel slot in the register. She shrugged.

"Isn't it open right now?" the girl asked. "My brother drove me over from Premont because you guys are the only store selling the real stars. We're getting one for his car, one for my parents' and some for our neighbors."

"Well—" Chon began. Ana turned toward the girl.

"Listen, little girl," she said, "he has to count the money in the drawer and put the total in the machine to close the last shift's totals. It'll take five minutes tops. But if you keep interrupting him, he won't be able to finish, and we won't sell you any damn stars. Understand?" Ana took the pack of Best Values from her purse and pulled out a smoke and her lighter.

Chon counted the pennies quickly, added the drawer total, and ran the numbers. The printout he put in an envelope with her credit card receipts said Ana's drawer was forty cents over. He input the total as his starting balance and rang up five John stars.

"Alright, sweetie," he said to the girl, who was staring at her feet, "$25."

The girl gave him two twenties. He gave her back three fives.

"You didn't have to—" he began to tell Ana.

"I know," she said.

"She was just trying to—"

"I know. It's just I see a little girl like that, all happy and shit, and I want to shake her. I want to fucking strangle her, it just hurts so fucking much."

Chon didn't say anything. He walked to the back room, slid the envelope under the office door to be counted along with the rest of the week's receipts by Sammy Alba, Art's cousin, tomorrow, like on every Monday.

Ana was standing at the front of the store, watching the girl from Premont tell her brother what had happened in the store.

"Ha," she said, "he flipped me off." She stood there, looking at the dust kicked up by the brother and his sister and the car that would carry them to their loving home three towns over. "We're out of Bud Light tall boys and Miller Lite caguamas," she said. "And four of the microwave burritos were cut into. I think Rocha did it when he opened up the box. I bagged them, they're in the cooler, leave a note for Sammy so he can write them off and order more beer."

"Okay, Ana. Thanks," Chon said.

Ana turned around and looked at him.

"Sometimes I just want to fucking scream. Hell, sometimes I do. I get home and I call detectives and call Bill and I cry. And then I get two days off, and I'm too sad to even go to Flojo's so I sit at home and drink and cry and, sometimes, I scream." She gave a laugh. She always laughed at awkward moments. "I'll see you Wednesday," she said.

"Well, I'll be here if you want to drop in," Chon said. A month ago, she might have taken him up on the offer—showed up on her day off with leftovers and helped him mop the store or stock the cooler.

"I'll see you Wednesday, Chon-Chon," she said walking out of the store.

She stood in the doorway trying to light her cigarette. When the wind wouldn't let her, she crouched down in the corner made by the ice machine and the storefront. Small as she was, she disappeared from Chon's sight. She could have been crying or curling up in a ball to give up on life or crawling away in the thirty seconds she was down there.

She popped up, cigarette lit, waved goodbye to Chon, and walked around the side of The Pachanga to get to her car. In the drive-thru window, Chon saw a woman tired and alone and who, in a bigger city, would fit right in pushing around a shopping cart and screaming at traffic passing by. She honked her horn when she pulled onto Main, waving at Chon with the back of her hand.

The John stars were Ms. Salinas' idea. The Mejias were left with some debt after the funeral. Keeping up with the Robison's arrangements was no easy task. Andres refused any of Arn's offered money to bridge the gap. Julie had life insurance policies on herself and Andres and had even taken one out on John, but it was a minimal thing—who can ever foresee having to pay for the funeral of your youngest son? Who would want to? Everyone in town knew of the Mejia's financial problems, so Ms. Salinas took action. What better way for the boys' teacher to get over her own grief than by helping out?

Ms. Salinas brought up the idea of selling car magnets—stars, like the Johns were and would have been—to raise funds to erase the Mejias' debt. They agreed—so long as the money made from such a venture would be split evenly with the Robisons. Arn had reservations about accepting any such money but didn't object because he knew his agreement on the matter would be the only way he and Angie could help Andres and Julie.

The magnets were bought at a discount from Ms. Salinas' cousin, the owner of a copy shop in Laredo, who informed her of the fact that the color burnt orange is trademarked by the University of Texas and, as such, could not be used commercially. So it was decided that Greenton High's spearmint green would do as the color for the stars, which read "JOHNS 3:16."

Art Alba was the only storeowner in town who initially agreed to sell the stars profit-free. When the other stores caught wind of his offer and changed theirs to match, Andres Mejia told them they could all fuck themselves and made The Pachanga the exclusive handler of the stars.

The funeral costs were recouped after a week. The Mejias and Robisons, when they saw that the sale of the stars was not likely to soon die down, decided that all the proceeds would go to a charity.

They had discussed giving the money to UT, but what for? The school had more money than it needed and hadn't regarded with wonder and awe the Johns the way the Johns had regarded UT. Then there was the Bee County hospital that had treated the boys. But it was agreed by all four parents, without being said by any of them, that the hospital that couldn't save their boys could burn to the ground for all they cared—and this was also their sentiment regarding the rural ambulance company that responded to the accident. Angie Robison suggested Greenton High and they all agreed. The dirty business of wiping their hands clean of the profits made by the memory of their dead sons was complete. The money would buy new uniforms for the baseball team.

Fake stars were popping up in the surrounding counties, one or two actually surfacing in Greenton. They were shoddy replications. Ms. Salinas' cousin in Laredo had made a simple but distinguishing augmentation to the shade of Greenton's spearmint green, which lightened it a bit. The counterfeiters couldn't seem to duplicate this. Some people were even coming into The Pachanga and purchasing scores of stars to sell at a marked-up price in counties farther away to people who were sympathetic to Greenton's loss. The Mejias and Robisons, it would seem, were alone in their compunction regarding profiting from the deaths of two teenagers.

Chon was helping a customer, a man in a black Mercedes that had overheated, when Henry walked in.

"Well, sir, we have a water hose at the side of the building that you can use to cool your car down before you put the coolant in," Chon said, giving Henry a nod. Henry gave him a nod back and walked to the soda fountain in the back of the store.

"But you're not supposed to take off the radiator cap when the car is hot," the tall man in khaki shorts and polo T-shirt said. Chon could tell the guy was a Mexican national from his accent and his clothes.

"Well, not really, but you've been parked for a while. We can be careful when we open it." Chon tried to speak slowly, breathing out through his nose—the way the training video Art had all of his employees watch instructed in dealing with elderly and mentally challenged customers and armed robbers. "Listen, sir, I'm just trying to get you out of here as soon as possible. You keep saying you're in a hurry."

"Fine, fine," the man said. "So we cool it with the water and fill it with coolant, but won't some water stay in the radiator?"

"Well, yeah, but that's fine. It'll just dilute the coolant a little bit, but it's totally fine," Chon said, looking back at Henry who was calling the guy a jerk off with his hand.

"No. The manual says to only put 50/50 coolant in the radiator, no water," the man said, putting his car's manual on the counter and giving a chortle as if to tell this kid that there are complexities of German engineering that he would never comprehend.

Chon let the sarcasm roll off his back. He had become near immune to assholes of all nationalities.

"Alright then, you'll want four gallons of coolant. They're across from the Pepsi cooler in the back," he said.

The man made his way to the automotive section. As he walked up the last aisle, Henry walked down the first—smiling and shaking his head the whole way. He leaned against the ice cream cooler and crossed his arms. Chon showed Henry the palm of his hand and gave him a nod. Just wait.

"$13.99?" the man yelled from the back of the store.

Chon smiled at Henry, who tried to hold back a laugh.

"You people charge $13.99 for a gallon of coolant?" The man came back to the counter with two gallon jugs of the stuff.

"Yes sir, it comes out to $15 a pop after taxes," Chon said, giving the man his back to Windex and squeegee the window behind the register.

"That's bullshit," the man said.

Chon turned around and scanned the jugs. "Well, sir, I don't set the prices here. I just ring stuff up and make change. But, I mean, you're kind of in the middle of a desert. There are towns and houses and stuff, but you see the sand and the cacti? That means you're in a desert."

"So you're going to be a smartass now?" the man said.

"No, I guess I'm just making excuses for my boss. Anyway, it'll just be the two of these?" Chon asked.

"Yes, that'll be it."

"So you're going to risk putting the water in? Because the first gallon and a half of coolant will evaporate and be sucked into the car, you'll need at least four gallons of coolant to top your car off." Chon pointed at the man's car in front of the store. He was feeling big—in control, like he was winning some respect from the man or at least evening a score between them that wasn't being kept—until he looked at the car. The wheels, dirty from not having been washed in a while, were of a quality that Chon had never seen in a town where driving in luxury was a brand new truck with a Flowmaster exhaust system or a Lincoln or Caddy that one of the town's retirees spent all of their squirreled-away money on and only drove to the post office and back. The curves of the car, its tinted windows and ultra bright headlights, fit the iconic hood ornament perfectly. Chon had seen it on TV or in magazines so many times that he hadn't thought seeing the real thing would come as such a shock. But it did. He wanted to walk outside and touch it—to feel what it was made of and complete the sensory experience.

"Well, whatever," the man said. "How much is it?" He looked at the number on the register, pulled out his wallet, and let a hundred fall down to the counter in front of Chon. Chon gave the man his change. The man walked out of the store to his car. He popped the hood and sat reading his car's manual in its dome light glow.

"What an asshole," Henry said.

Chon stood looking out at the man sitting in his car. He threw a towel at Henry.

"Go help him," he said.

"Me? I don't work here. Let him figure it out," Henry said, turning around to see what the guy would do.

"Man, I told him to open his radiator and flush it with water. He's probably going to burn himself. You know he doesn't know what he's doing," Chon said.

"Well, why don't you go help him then," Henry asked. He looked back at his friend and seemed to get something.

"Fine," Henry said, and walked out of the store.

Chon watched Henry go and talk to the man, who had tried to open the hood just as Henry walked over to get the nozzled water hose from the side of the store. Henry found the latch the man hadn't been able to. Using the towel to protect his hand and forearm from the steam that would issue forth, Henry opened the radiator and proceeded to spray water into it to cool it down.

"The dumb asshole's radiator cap wasn't screwed on right. He must have smarted off, private school-style, at the last guy who changed his fluids," Henry said, drying his hands with a paper towel. "You could have helped him, you know."

Chon had mopped the store up in the time it took Henry to help the man. "Yeah, I know. But I had him. I made him look like the asshole he was. How am I going to turn around and help him outside when I just won inside?"

"Won what?" Henry asked. "The guy was trying to buy some coolant to fill his car. Sure, he was an asshole. Sure, you made him look like more of an asshole. But what did you win when he didn't even know he was playing your little game? You got him, but he didn't even know he was gotten. You think he's even going to remember you tomorrow, or even me?"

Chon shook his head and scanned an 18-pack of beer. "Give me some money," he said.

Henry handed him a twenty. "My tip for helping the businessman from Tamaulipas," he said.

Chon paid the money into the register and put the change and the beer on the counter.

"I know we're not being taped," Henry said, looking up at a shot of himself from behind on the TV monitor above the counter, "but it still feels weird seeing myself on this monitor."

"That's the point," Chon said, waiting for his register totals to print out. "That's why they don't even bother recording anything. Watching yourself do something wrong is enough to make you think twice about doing it."

Chon put the printout in an envelope and slid it under the office door. "You know so much about this store," he said, standing in the doorway, Henry waiting for him to lock up the shop, "that if we ever break up, I'll have to kill you."

"Shit," Henry said, "I'm only with you for your car."

They got in the Dodge-nasty and rode silently, with the windows down, a dry breeze rolling into the car. It was a nice enough night, by Greenton's hot standard. It had reached 103° earlier that day. Another night wasted drinking beer and watrching TV with Henry didn't seem too bad a prospect, because what else was there to do?

When they arrived at Henry's house, Chon noticed a Suburban parked where he would otherwise have parked his car if he were coming to pick up Henry. He raised an eyebrow at Henry.

"They've been hanging out and drinking and talking about Mejia and my cousin like they had already been married or something," Henry said, looking at his uncle's Suburban. "He'll be there all night and pass out on the couch. My dad's trying to be cool, but he has to work in the morning—alone, because my uncle won't show up. My dad's getting annoyed with this, it's almost every night. Fuck it. Let's just ride around."

Chon veered left at the Y, the place in South Greenton where Main forks and becomes Smith Street going southwest toward Zapata and Fal Street going east toward Falfurrias. The night was cooler than usual. Summer's end approached. But autumn's crawl into town wouldn't bring any leaves changing colors, fluttering down from trees. There would be no cold snaps and little or no call for scarves and earmuffs or thick jackets. Chon would be back in school—that was autumn in Greenton. Back to a place like a prison, sitting in a room full of people who shared the same insecurities and desires but who were too self-absorbed, too teenaged, to notice that everyone else felt exactly the same.

In a week Chon would return to school for the last nine months of his sentence, but he would do it with a mission and a hidden smile.

He turned the car right onto Old Cemetery and parked, rolling his window down while Henry pulled out two beers from the case in the backseat. Chon opened his beer and took a pull. Henry turned on the Dodge-nasty's radio. On certain nights, radio stations drifted into Greenton from San Antonio. On days when storms were blowing in, stations could be picked up from Houston or Mexico. Chon leaned back on the headrest and closed his eyes, letting a satisfying belch come up slowly and feeling the day's work roll off his shoulders while Henry moved the radio's dial through white noise and evangelists. He even skipped some good songs in search of foreign frequencies bringing in brief bands of new, cool, hip elsewhere.

Henry opened his beer and took a drink. "One more week, man. One more week and it's back to that goddamn hole," he said, looking out of his window at the ditch as if he'd heard a scuttle. "I don't care how much my father needs my help at work. I'm just going to drink beer and watch TV and sleep till noon between now and then—if I can get a beer from the goddamn fridge before Araceli's father drinks them all."

"So he's there like every night?" Chon turned the radio up a notch.

"Pretty much, with my aunt out of town," Henry said, taking another drink.

"So, when's she getting back?" Chon asked. He tried to crush his empty beer can, but only bent in one side, pinching his hand nearly to the point of bleeding. He grabbed another, opened it, and had his first sip before he looked over at Henry who was staring directly at him, waiting for his eyes. It startled Chon. He thought his nonchalance was sufficient cover for the interrogation.

"Listen, man. I'm not going to help you out," he said, then put his beer on the dash in front of him. "I've never had to bring it up because Mejia was always in the way, but now…I'm not going to help you with my cousin."

Chon made to speak, but Henry cut him off.

"I mean, I knew it was going to come up, and if that's not what was happening just now, I apologize. But even if that's not what you were doing, you eventually would. My aunt left last week for Corpus to bring Araceli back home. She'll stay there with her best friend, the one Araceli stayed with all summer. They'll all go to the beach and shop for school clothes and try to not think of Greenton or any of the bullshit here. Then at the end of the week, my aunt will come back with Araceli so she can finish school. That's what I know and that's all I'll tell you. After that, bro, you're on your own."

Chon looked over at Henry, then at the sky out Henry's window. Lightning traced faint blue branches across the sky over Falfurrias in the distance. The storm's rains were flirting with the smell of Greenton's dry-cracked orange dirt and with Chon's senses and his need for the doom-jazz mood of a rainy night. He drained his beer for lack of anything to say and came up coughing before the bottom of the can.

Henry grabbed a couple of beers and got out of the car. Chon opened a new beer and followed Henry.

"So that's it, right? We don't need to talk about this again?"

"Fine by me," Chon said.

Henry nodded and looked over the cemetery at the storm in the distance. "Why do you think rain only ever comes to the edge of town?" he asked. "It's like, nine out of every ten storms that come by stay out of town. Isn't that weird?"

"Would you want to come to this town, even to visit, if you didn't have to?" Chon said.

"No, but it's not like the rain stays somewhere better. Falfurrias and Benavides suck too."

"But they're not here," Chon said.

"You know, people have been sneaking into the cemetery at night to visit their graves," Henry said. "My dad and uncle came over all drunk the other night and saw some people."

"Place looks empty to me," Chon said.

"Well, yeah. It's Sunday."

"So they've been sneaking in and what, just hanging out?"

"I guess. You wanna go?" Henry asked.

"Why would I want to sneak into the cemetery?"

"Why would you want to park your goddamn car next to a cemetery in the middle of the night? Because there ain't shit else to do."

Chon shook his head at this. He couldn't argue so solid a point if he tried.

"And to see them," Henry added. "You don't have to be all sad and obsessed like everyone else in this town—all morbid and weird and shit. But it's also kind of strange that you haven't come by to see them. Before whatever the fuck you think happened happened, they were people you knew. People you played with. People who are dead."

"And what? Seeing them will help me heal or something like that?" Chon asked

"How the fuck would I know? But at least you'll have gone." Henry put his two extra beers in the back pockets of his jeans and waded into the knee-high dried whitish-brown grass. He cut a path through the ditch and around the cemetery fence with such confidence that Chon was certain he'd been to visit the Johns already this summer. Chon rolled his eyes and followed. Henry got to a post that Chon would not have noticed was severed of its connection to the dozen or so bottom links of fence. He pulled up the fence and, with a practiced agility Chon wouldn't have expected of his big clumsy friend, duck-walked under.

"I can't believe I'm sneaking into a cemetery," Chon said, handing his beer under the fence to Henry and getting down on his hands and knees to crawl through the break. "So what..." Chon said, pulling dry dirt burrs from his hands when he got to the other side, "people cut a back entrance to the fence so they could be with their Johns whenever they need a fix of late night what-might-have-been?"

"No, they've been hopping the fence. I did this myself when I was little. So I could be with my mom."

Chon took his beer from Henry, had a drink, and looked up at the full moon's bright pale glow for something to say. It gave back nothing, only a bluish white light. It looked and felt like New Year's Eves gone by when, as a child, Chon learned that night's scary dark could be painted fun by phosphorus, magnesium, and copper burning bright in the sky and by the moon that glowed through the gun smoke left hanging in the air.

Henry spoke up. "I used to ride my bike out here and just sit. Sometimes I'd talk. Sometimes I wouldn't say anything because I knew she knew exactly what I was feeling and thinking. I would come because I was scared. I was always real scared when I was little, and my mom would let me come to her bedroom to sleep on the floor by her bed. After she died, my dad would let me crash on the bed. But it was different. It didn't feel, or even smell, the same. So I took to not bothering. I'd just stay up scared and, when it got to where I couldn't take it, I'd sneak out here. I still come out a lot, but not at night anymore."

"Did you ever see anyone else trying to sneak in?"

"No, but every now and then the sun wouldn't wake me up and the gravedigger would find me. He'd throw my bike in the hearse and drive me home. He never told my dad."

"Wow," was all Chon could say.

"Fucked up, huh?" Henry said, walking with the perfect balance of a high-beam construction worker, not looking back at Chon, taking care not to step on any graves, bending over to right fallen vases or wreaths without breaking his stride.

"This is it," he said when they got to the adjacent graves.

Chon looked down. Even in the moonlight, he could see the strange outline the recently laid sod cut into the surrounding dirt and dead grass. For all of their exultation in life, Chon expected the Johns would have gotten something more than slabs of granite identical to all of the other slabs around them save for their jersey numbers—8 for Mejia, 34 for Robison—engraved in the upper right-hand corner.

Chon pursed his lips into a tight frown and stuck his chin out. He nodded, as if appraising the work of the stonemason who made the headstones. He drank down the last of his beer and dropped the can to the ground.

Henry picked up the can, placed it on a large rock on the caliche cemetery drive in front of the graves, stomped it flat and put it in his pocket. "You know, they're not the only people from this shit hole who've ever died. The whole town seems to think so, even you. You act like this is the goddamn John Cemetery and all the other people here were just test runs or something. The sooner everyone in town realizes that these are just two guys who died, the better. And it sucks—they could play ball, and they were going to make it and put us on the map or whatever. They have families who miss them—not the futures they were going to have. But they died like everyone else here, and the grass on their graves is going to die and in a few months their graves will look like all the others. Until Greenton realizes that, we're going to live in a goddamn circus."

Chon looked at the Johns' graves, then at the rows of the other ones that held Greenton's departed. There were statues big and small, the Virgen and St. Jude the most prominent among them after Christ. There were headstones pink, grey, and black; double and single; with hinge-shut peepholes that revealed faded pink and yellow photos of the dead. Chon imagined that they were like the photos his parents had at home of different family outings, always with kids slamming away at a piñata, always one of the cousins crying.

There were empties next to graves—some brown-bag special tallboys, some amber glass long necks. He could even see an Oso Negro. They were the remnants of the daily or weekly catch-up sessions between the survivors and the hallowed ground they came to talk to, to cry on, to seek comfort from in the middle of the night.

Lightning flashed in the east and a cool, damp air blew in.

"I'm gonna go see my mom," Henry said. Before he left, he pulled a beer out of his back left pocket and handed it to Chon. He opened the other and held it up in the cool air.

Chon cracked open his beer.

"Here's to coming to see off the Johns," he said. "And seeing everyone." Neither he nor Henry made to tap their drinks. Arm still held out, Chon added, "God bless them."

Henry nodded and they drank. He turned on his heel and had already taken two steps away from Chon in the time it took Chon to bring the drink to his mouth.

The pull he took of the beer tasted off. The beers had gotten warm enough in the backseat of the Dodge-nasty, but adding the heat of Henry Monsevais' sweaty ass on the other side of a layer of denim and cotton and the shaking they got from his crawling and walking, Chon's seemed to have gone flat.

He looked in the direction Henry had gone, but he couldn't see him, just diagonal rows of headstones that met at the road like a series of arrows pointing at Chon. He was tired and hadn't had a proper dinner. His stomach was aching from the beer. The breeze picked up and the sweat at Chon's hairline tingled, making his ears feel cold.

Odd that he didn't feel scared or anxious. He felt himself, a man—a boy—alive and alone among so many people who were cut off from consciousness and worry, existing unaffected by all of the sadness of the world.

Mejia owed Chon nothing. If the two of them had ever really competed at or for anything—and Chon could admit now that, outside of Little League baseball, they hadn't—no score that existed between them mattered anymore. If Mejia had ever laid claim to Araceli, a claim that could only be valid in reciprocity, that claim was now not only nullified, but nonexistent. So too was Chon's anger and resentment toward Mejia.

Chon let go. Even he could see that if what he had felt could be so easily unfelt, it probably meant that he had been grasping at straws. Letting even that go was a relief to Chon. He could proceed without anger or negativity guiding him.

Chon caught sight of Henry sitting beside a grave a few rows back of the road, pulling weeds that had sprouted up. He looked down at the Johns' graves and poured half of his beer out for Mejia and the other half for Robison. Just like in life, his actions went undetected by the Johns—that made Chon smile. He didn't register to them. They were on a totally different plane, and that put many things inside of Chon Gonzales at peace.

To the east, rain that Greenton so desperately needed had fallen and was being soaked up by Falfurrias' own thirsty soil. In the morning, Greentonites would wake up to the same hot temperatures that they'd faced the day before. Most of them would not know about the storm that had flirted with the city limit sign or the brief cool it blew through the Greenton Cemetery.

Araceli Monsevais arrived in Greenton the same way she left—secretly and in the hope of evading the teary gazes and unmitigated sorrow of Greentonites. Greenton seemed the same to her, which struck her initially as odd. It reminded her of something she'd thought about in catechism when they told her time doesn't pass in heaven. Or how they said in physics that time is relative. She figured maybe it would stop existing when she did. She hadn't necessarily thought Greenton would cease existing when she left it, but the fact of it existing so very much without change made her think that it was a place existing on a timeless plane, not unlike heaven, but probably closer to hell.

In the passenger seat of her mother's idling car, at the only stoplight in town, Araceli counted a silent one...two...three...four... Exactly on five, the light turned green. Purgatory, she decided. It was like purgatory, but smaller.

It was late, after midnight, on the night before the first day of school. Town was almost as dead as a child expects the world to be in the small hours between goodnight prayers and the sound of mom's voice calling her to wake up. The late arrival wasn't any kind of precaution Araceli and her mother had planned. They were held up by a long parting in Corpus with the Vela family, people who seemed fonder of Araceli than she was of them. They felt they had taken her in like one would a wounded puppy. Araceli, though, felt like a teenager forced to spend her last summer in high school with strangers.

Her mother didn't decide immediately to send Araceli to the Velas' for the summer. It wasn't until she called her husband at work and he went into hysterics that she realized her daughter would have to be protected from what was going to happen all over town. Her mother decided to give her daughter time and space so that she could process the loss of John Mejia, whose friendship and shared time made him something more than a childhood love, something like a brother to Araceli—a boy whose fears and insecurities only she knew, like only she knew how ticklish he was behind his right knee and how sometimes he would wake up in the middle of the night after having dreams about striking out or missing his mark on a deep pass, leading Greenton High to a loss and Greenton proper to great disappointment and anger.

She didn't resent her parents for sending her to Corpus. She was grateful she didn't have to go to the Johns' funeral, and that she wasn't part of the town-wide craziness that she'd gotten almost nightly doses of over the phone. Half, or less, of that craziness was relayed by her mother, trying her best to be as delicate and considerate of what her daughter was going through as she could. She had to tell her the truth about the wreck Araceli's father had become at the loss of the son-in-law he would never have.

The most news, however, came from the house Araceli used to sneak into and out of most nights so that she could be with the person she honestly believed she would be with for the rest of her life.

Julie Mejia didn't call Araceli on the day the Johns died. She left that, like so much else, to Goyo, who called the Monsevais house himself. When Araceli picked up, he asked her in a calm tone to give the phone to one of her parents. When she saw the look on her mother's face, she remembered thinking that nothing that had been reported could hit her as hard as it hit her mother. And, aside from the kick of the initial shock, Araceli was right.

Araceli was not, however, mourning the loss of any plans to be with John Mejia after high school. A rift had formed between the couple when John returned from a visit to Austin. He and Robison had toured the campus, had taken a few very unofficial swings at the Longhorn practice facility. Mejia was given what he called—in defense of his stupidity—a "dry and painful" handjob from a drunken coed at a party in the apartment of a red-shirt sophomore pitcher from Brenham. She'd cried tears over their relationship then—they both had. Against her better judgment and in a desperate attempt to hold onto the place she'd forged for herself in Greenton, Araceli took him back. But it was never the same.

He began talking a lot more about the future, but her role in John's plans seemed a peripheral one. He would mention being in school and playing ball and hoping for a future in pro ball and, after that, in coaching. The *I* became more pronounced as the *we* seemed to shrink on the horizon until Araceli was left behind like all of Greenton would soon be.

She didn't mention it, but, after he and Robison signed their commitment letters with UT, the end of their relationship hung on and around every minute they spent together. She told John that 'commitment letters' sounded funny to her, like some sort of pre-nuptial agreement he had made with the university. He laughed, but she saw that it was something much more meaningful and romantic to him. Officially joining the ranks of Roger Clemens and Burt Hooton and Spike Owen—cementing it in ink, on 25# paper, with all of Greenton and much of South Texas watching in person and on TV—was the biggest moment of John Mejia's life. And while she was there, it was a moment not really involving Araceli, as they almost all would be from then on.

That silently acknowledged inevitability arose every time John mentioned the time they would spend apart during his freshman and her senior year or his probable start in the minors, living out of a bag on the road, in buses, playing to half-filled stadiums in

Bumfuck, all in hopes of being mined up ahead of the other prospects on the field by a big league team—living the dream. She suffered the obvious with feigned indifference, a cold stoicism that seemed to hurt Mejia more than the fact that soon he would break the heart of the only person he'd ever loved.

The night before he and Robison left town—the night before they died—John took Araceli as far away from the party lights at the Saenz ranch as its boundaries let him. He drove his father's truck along a dirt path that led around the perimeter of the property, stopping a few miles away when they reached a locked gate.

John turned off the engine. He and Araceli got out of the truck and climbed onto a blanket John laid out on its bed. They didn't say a word. When they finished, she wrapped the blanket around them. John cried silently on her chest, his tears rolling up to her collarbone and down off her back. Araceli lay counting stars, certain that this was the end, determined not to break down with him.

The next day, on the front lawn of his parents' house, John Mejia broke up with Araceli Monsevais. Right there in front of everyone. "We have to break up," he said. A few tears fell, but as soon as Araceli felt them coming, she steeled herself and stopped. He held her and whispered to her that he would always love her and be her friend. He told her he still wanted her to go to UT when she graduated, to be with him. He said he would call her every day and asked her to please look after his mother which, last-minute public breakup or not, she knew wasn't asking too much.

All of Greenton watched, oblivious to the fact that their king and queen were a couple no longer. She told herself that she'd known it was coming, but still it hurt like she thought a gunshot might. Araceli was proud that she hadn't cried, that she hadn't done something foolish like making an angry scene.

Riding back into town on the night before the start of the school year, Araceli remembered what hurt her most that day: the realization—as the Johns drove off with their police escort and the whole town cheering them on—that with Greenton's king leaving town, she was no longer its queen. She was just a girl. Maybe she was more beautiful than the girls around her, but she was no longer any more special or remarkable than all of the prettiest girls in school who had come before her—girls who only ever seemed to get married and pregnant and fat, left with picture books and school annuals to show kids who don't really care that their mothers were young once too, that they used to be beautiful.

FALL

School started on a Wednesday. Chon woke up early, not as tired as he should have been. Sammy Alba was taking advantage of the last days of Chon's daytime availability and had scheduled him to work open to three on both Monday and Tuesday. Rocha was taking advantage of Chon working that shift on Tuesday too because he didn't show up the night before. He called Sammy, and even Art in San Antonio, he claimed, but neither answered. Chon tried getting hold of Ana, but she didn't answer, as had become her practice on her days off, especially now since Chon had stopped coming over. Chon did some half-hearted sulking and moaning to himself during his second shift at The Pachanga, but couldn't get into it as, in the dead minutes and hours between customers, his mind wandered constantly to Araceli and the excitement of seeing her the next day.

After the floors were swept and mopped, the cash in the register dropped into the one-way slot in the floor safe, his paperwork slid under the office door, Chon turned off the lights and locked the store up for the night. At home, his sleep was uneasy, restless.

When he woke up the next morning, though he had already done so the night before, Chon showered. This was unlike him, and his parents noted it.

"Pito's not even this excited about his first day of school," his mother said.

Chon ignored her, hoping that the real reason he was so excited wouldn't be apparent to his parents or his brother—and certainly not to his classmates. Because what would that make him in their eyes? A predator? An opportunist? Chon wasn't ready to recognize that in himself, much less in the angry, judging eyes of everybody within the walls of Greenton High—from its students to its teachers and administrators, to even its two janitors and three lunch ladies.

He put on the new clothes his parents bought him and the Polo boots and Seiko watch, plus a dab of the cologne he had bought on a trip the family took to the mall in Laredo. He looked at himself in the mirror. The pricey acne medication he had also bought on that trip was working. His face was clearing, pockmarked and scarred, but no longer oily and red. The bedroom push-ups, backyard weight lifting, and daily glasses of chalky whey protein shakes he'd been drinking were bulking him up, little by little. On a good day, like this one, Chon could see the image before him in the shiny glass and let himself believe that he wasn't too bad looking.

Maybe, just maybe, there was a chance.

Chon left the bathroom and made three tacos of the chorizo and egg his mother had woken up early to make. She didn't do this often. Chon usually got breakfast on the way to school with his own money. Usually Pito was planted sleepily on a chair at the family dining table with a bowl of cereal in front of him and the morning's news playing on the TV. This was a big day however. It was Chon's first day of his senior year of high school and Pito's first day at Greenton Junior High.

Chon wrapped the tacos in a paper towel and walked to the door. Pito though was only halfway through his breakfast.

"We leave now, or you walk," Chon said.

"Concepcion." His mother only ever called him by his proper name in reproach. "Be nice."

"Yeah, Concepcion," Pito said, mocking.

"Guadalupe, you listen to your brother," their mother said, getting up and meeting the boys at the door. "I love you guys." She gave each of them a kiss on the cheek. "Be good."

Chon and Pito sat, letting the Dodge-nasty's engine warm up. Pito interrupted Chon's reverie.

"Do you think today will be weird?" Pito asked.

"It's just another day at school. Only you're at a bigger campus with lockers and bells ringing every period and dressing out for gym."

"No," Pito said. "I mean at your school. This will be the first day of school after it happened. It'll be the first time everyone sees Araceli. Don't you think that'll be weird?"

Foolishly, in all of Chon's planning and scheming over this day, he had never factored in what he knew had to be waiting at school, even though the frenzy had died down a bit. The church had stopped sending its statue of the weeping virgin from house to house so that every believing, willing family would say a novena for the Johns. *The View*, Greenton's weekly, five-page news circular was no longer running stories about the Johns or at least had begun relegating them—now mainly responses to letters to the editor—to the back page of the paper. While folks were still coming into The Pachanga and buying John stars, they no longer did so weepingly or out of grief, but acquisitively and in line with the trend running through town.

Pito was right though. This was the first day all the teenagers in Greenton would be in one place—within the walls of the high school which were adorned by so many trophies and banners won by the fallen heroes, where they had walked and studied and presided as the ultimate alpha dogs, held in high esteem by even the teachers and administrators.

These same adolescents would focus all of their collective sadness on Araceli. Chon realized he would never get her attention, never get her away from the watchful gaze of almost a tenth of the people in town.

"Whatever. They can get over it," he told his little brother.

"Yeah, but they won't get over it today," Pito said. "It seems like no one ever will. They were—" he stopped here, either because he couldn't put into words what the Johns meant to the town or to him. Or because he knew Chon wasn't listening to him.

Chon dropped Pito off at the junior high, a WPA-era building erected to look like a fallout shelter and a factory for the crop-cut future GIs who would come up in the last pure, pre-rock 'n' roll era of American youth. You could almost hear Hank Williams tunes hanging in the air of the parking lot of what was initially Greenton High, with its vomit-hued green and pink tiles and cracked speaker box intercom system. At least it had windows, which is more than could be said for the new Greenton High, built like a high-security prison with cinderblock-walls and fluorescent lights.

When he got to the high school parking lot, he sat for a while behind the wheel of the Dodge-nasty, day dreaming. The loud mock-childish whine of a DJ in some cramped booth in Laredo coming through the radio snapped Chon out of his trance. He killed the ignition and got out of the car, not bothering to lock its doors or even roll up its windows. He saw two girls in front of school break down and cry at the sight of each other and rush into an embrace right there in the student parking lot. *Ohhhh.* It was going to be a long year.

The crying girls walked into the school building, arm in arm. In front of the school, the sun had only risen partially in the eastern sky, but the lack of trees or buildings to block out its rays made the day bright and already hot. Chon saw only his own reflection in the glass doors at the entrance. He readied himself for chaos on the other side—a building full of people falling all over each other, seeing who could wail the loudest or who had the best story about the Johns—but there no one to be found. In fact, the entrance hall, which was flanked on either side by the school's main office and library, was barer than Chon had ever seen it. So too was the main hall. A note was taped to the office door: an assembly in the gym would start at 8:50 am.

Every student in school was there, sitting on one side of the gym bleachers. Teachers were standing, doing the business of corralling students and having them sit in sections according to grade level. Each grade had about sixty students, except for the senior class, which had only fifty-two. They had started out with sixty-seven, but eight had moved away, six had dropped out to work or dedicate their lives to various drugs of choice, and one had been arrested trying to sneak a few pounds of weed from Mexico through the Sarita checkpoint just up the highway.

Chon had gone to school with most of these kids since kindergarten. He would know them forever. He just hoped that he wouldn't have to spend the rest of his life with them.

Chon scanned the rows of seniors as soon as he entered the gym. Only Araceli was missing. Chon took a seat next to Henry, who was sitting alone, only two ass-lengths away from the nearest person—close enough to make small talk, but not close enough to commit himself to any clique or conversation.

"This is gonna be a fucked up year, man," Henry said, giving Chon a pound on the shoulder when he sat. "It's all going to be this day, just a little different, for the whole year. I guarantee it."

Chon nodded his head in agreement, looking around the gym at all the teenagers in town. Seeing the home side of the gym barely halfway filled, Chon had one of those moments—*God, Greenton was small.*

On the floor was a podium, no mic. They didn't need a mic. Behind the podium stood two veiled frames on easels.

"Oh Lord, did they do portraits or something?" Chon asked.

Henry shrugged and turned to say something to Chon. When he saw Chon scanning the rows of students and looking anxiously at the gym doors, he rolled his eyes.

"She's coming, man."

The door to the gym opened. Everyone turned to look. Araceli walked in wearing a new pair of jeans and a plain pink T-shirt. Her hair was pulled back. She wore no makeup or jewelry. All the other girls in the gym were decked out in clothes some of them had worked all summer to buy just for this day—not too low-cut blouses, summer skirts and dresses, new shoes and sandals. They had woken up very early that morning to wash and primp and preen. By comparison, Araceli looked like a girl who had shown up without a pencil to take a test that she didn't know was being given, in a subject she hadn't studied, written in a language she couldn't read.

But none of the other girls' attempts brought them any closer to the perfection Araceli achieved without trying. She was the essence of what Plato would have imagined if he tried to quantify the highest form of beauty. At least she was all Chon could imagine when he tried to do the same. It was the moment Chon had longed for, seeing Araceli walk back into Greenton High and back into his life. It was too brief, a moment that Chon couldn't focus on and savor like he would have wanted. His attention was diverted by the looks on the faces of his classmates and the anger he felt at the groups of students, pockets of them in all grade levels, obviously and tackily leaning over to whisper their speculations and theories, some of them even pointing as Araceli made her way to the other side of the gym.

When she started up the bleachers, her fellow cheerleaders began making room for her. They flashed big smiles her way, conveying with their eyes their deepest sympathies. Each one of them thought they shared a close bond with her because—unbeknownst to each other—they had all slept with John Robison at various points over the last few years. Araceli gave them an unsmiling, indifferent wave as she passed them by. They made no attempt to hide their shock. They turned around fully in their seats, watching her walk away with looks that towed the line between hurt and contempt.

Araceli continued up the bleachers, getting bigger and sharper and closer to real life as she drew nearer, the entire student body of Greenton High making her a show and a spectacle. Chon didn't know if he was angrier at them for doing this to her when she had already gone through so much or because the hungry look in their eyes implicated him so greatly. They looked ready to pounce, wanting to be her friends, her lovers, to be close to her.

But they didn't want her like Chon did. Chon believed that. They just wanted to get close to celebrity—as much a celebrity as Greenton had right then and would maybe ever have again. But he wanted the girl, a girl he had wanted for so long, who was no different now for having lost her boyfriend or for having left Greenton under cover of night.

Araceli walked past the last group of students sitting on the bleachers. Choosing to sit alone on the top row of bleachers would baffle everyone writing the narrative of the return of Araceli Monsevais in their heads. It would be endlessly discussed at school and reported to curious parents and siblings at home who had as much invested in the storyline as anyone else.

Walking balance-beam style on the lowest unpopulated bench, she cut a path over to where Chon was sitting. His heart rate quickened. The muscles in his arms and legs grew tight. All the thoughts about Araceli in his dreams crashed in the face of Araceli in the flesh. He felt the distinct sensation of being pulled back down to earth, one which felt strikingly similar to realizing that you are full of shit. What could he ever really say to her? What profound and insightful statement could he make to cut to the core of her soul and endear her to him forever? What cool, funny quip to make her laugh or smile? What squeak, cough, or bark could he utter, just then, to let her know he existed?

It didn't matter. She stopped one person short of him—one big person—sitting down next to Henry, giving her cousin a more sincere hug than Chon had ever seen her give. That hug transformed Henry in Chon's eyes from his goofy best friend—someone Chon regarded as something of a sidekick—into a man in his own right. Chon was awed, as was everyone else in the gym (except Henry), at the power Henry was given by Araceli grabbing him and then falling into the embrace he gave her.

Down on the gym floor, Mr. Adame tried to get the gym's attention by tapping on the podium, then knocking on it, then finally pounding it with the heel of his hand. He had been the principal for the last seven years. He was thirty-three years old.

"Ladies and gentlemen, your attention," he said.

"Would you look at this goofy fucking asshole?" Henry said. Chon and Araceli laughed and looked at each other with smiles.

Mr. Adame really did look like a goofy fucking asshole. Formerly a three-piece suit kind of guy, he stood at the podium in a pair of nut-hugging Wranglers, a bolo tie and pearl-button shirt, a twenty-gallon black felt hat, and an out-of-the-box pair of ostrich skin boots. He was raised in Houston, had come to Greenton fresh out of graduate school in College Station, going straight from a bachelor's program in secondary education to a master's program in school administration. Greenton High was the only principalship he could find that required no teaching experience. Though he believed wholeheartedly in the power and necessity of a good education, he hated children. No one—the students, their parents, the staff—had warmed to him over the last seven years. But this year was the year he had decided to connect with his students and the rural community they lived in.

"Good morning. And welcome to the first day of the '98-'99 school year. I hope you had a good restful summer and that you've come back to GHS ready and eager to learn and to take the necessary steps to become a success by the end of the term, the school year, and your respective graduation dates. I know this summer started out in a very strange way. We entered it in a way that has to be addressed here today."

Mr. Adame appeared to want for a stack of papers to shuffle. He looked down at the podium and brushed off a piece of dust or lint that wasn't there. Beads of sweat gathered on his forehead, just below the brim of his stupid hat.

"So. Here to talk to you is Ms. Salinas."

Henry blew a scoff through his nose, nodded in the direction of Mr. Adame, and said, "Mas puto que la chingada."

Henry couldn't write a paragraph or even conjugate most irregular verbs in Spanish, but in decrying a puto, he was Neruda.

Chon laughed and looked to Araceli, but she wasn't laughing. She seemed to dread what Ms. Salinas might say, as if it would call her out as being the integrity flaw on the wall of the tire that blew out on John Robison's Explorer. Chon caught her eyes and tried to give her a nod that reassured her that it would all be okay. He threw his shoulders into the nod however, and it came off as if he were mad-dogging her and giving her the nonverbal *what the fuck?* instead. Thankfully for Chon, she didn't seem to take in what he had done. She didn't regard it and try to make sense of it. His nod was a black cat on a grey sofa that she walked by in a dark room. It was in her line of sight, but her brain didn't catch it. Chon sighed. It was the last four years all over again.

Ms. Salinas grabbed the far corners of the podium in front of her, holding it like she was standing in a hurricane, and gave a loud "bleh," in lieu of screaming. Some of the students, mainly freshmen and sophomores, laughed.

"I've been away from here for two and a half months. Too long? Not long enough?" She almost shouted. "I don't know. I mean, I live two blocks away from here. I pass by here to get to Main. So pretty much any day I leave the house, I pass by here. I guess it was about a week ago that I stopped crying when I drove past." She covered her face with her hands.

A cold electricity filled the room, conducted by a collective drying of throats and chilling of spines and tightening of stomachs. Everyone shifted in their seats—shuffling their feet, straightening their postures, a few people pulling their knees to their shoulders.

"We teachers have been on campus for a week. If any of my colleagues are talking about what happened just less than three months ago, they're not talking about it with me. It's like they thought I wouldn't be able to deal. Even last night, when I laid out clothes and got mentally ready to start a new year with you guys, I didn't think about it. I lied to myself. Right now, standing in front of you all, I can't lie. To myself, I guess, but mainly to you. All week, we will have grief counselors here on campus. They're here to help us, ALL of us, to face what's happened. Because before we can deal with it, we have to face it. Do you understand?"

Ms. Salinas had been looking around the gym at everyone during her speech, but at that moment she fixed her gaze on Araceli, taking with her the eyes of everyone in the gym. But Araceli looked away, up at where ceiling and wall met to her right. She might have been rolling her watering eyes or trying not to cry.

Ms. Salinas clenched her jaw. "And so," she said, "that option is on the table." Eyes shifted away from Araceli to the podium. "We encourage you all to consider it. Take your grief seriously. I know there are some of you who weren't close with the Johns"—there it was— "but regardless of that, death has come into our town and death has taken two of our sons and brothers. You may not have planned on meeting him, but you know him now. That can be a lot to swallow. Talking about it helps."

Ms. Salinas stood looking hard and wide-eyed at the audience in front of her. No one said a word, their faces all blank. Disappointment trickled down her body, eroding the juts and peaks of eyebrows raised, lips stretched thin in anticipation, shoulders thrust forward as if to embrace. Were these kids too dumb to understand what she was talking about? It seemed they were.

She looked down, then back. She cleared her throat. "Alright, then. Starting with the freshmen, we'll all leave for homeroom. Just follow the teacher at the head of the section, and you'll get where you're going." She walked away from the podium like a zombie, tired and sad.

Everyone stood up. The classes started moving around and talking and acting like teenagers despite having met Death in all his uncaring dedication to the business he held most dear. Mr. Adame stepped back up to the podium.

"Now if you'll all wait, I have one more announcement to make." Everyone slowed down without stopping, talked out of the corners of their mouths instead of just being quiet. "Students!" he said louder, shouting.

"There will be an unveiling in front of the office after school. You're all invited, encouraged, to stay." He punctuated the last word with no cadence, left it hanging. He looked hard at the students he was paid to manage, the takers of tests whose results would make or break his career.

Feeling better for having made them wait, he dismissed them. "Have a good school year."

Chon felt like he could never approach Araceli after that assembly—not to give her his love and ask for hers back, not even to ask her for a pencil or sheet of paper to borrow. It wasn't like he was trying to steal her from her boyfriend, as had been the, in retrospect, hopeless plan before Chon's and Greenton's existences had been forever changed by a blown-out tire and a car with an unsafe center of gravity and weight placement. What he wanted to do was a good and right thing: love her, save her, help her. He'd just have to wait to do it until he could look her in the face without being dwarfed by all of her young, tragic wisdom.

They walked out of the gym together or, more accurately, each walked out with Henry— one on either side, each needing something different from him, each asking almost too much in their separate ways. Chon noted Araceli going into a government class down the hall from his world geography class. Afterward, he followed her to her trigonometry class. He had physics that period. Chon hurried out of his class and over two halls to see Araceli leave trigonometry and head for her next class, which ended up being in the same room he had just left. The physics teacher—a man who was noted in some history books and encyclopedias for having snuck into Viet Cong camps under cover of night and slit the throats of scores of men—also taught French. Chon had Spanish that period, his classroom clear on the other side of the small campus. As soon as the bell rang, Chon rushed out, walking as fast as he could without looking suspicious and made it over to the science hall in about a minute and a half. But Araceli was nowhere to be seen.

When he walked into his fourth period English class, Chon was thinking about how at least he knew what class Araceli would be in the period after—cheerleading, which met in the cafeteria—and how he could even go out of his way to walk by there before heading for his car and work at the Pachanga. He was so lost in his plans that he didn't notice until he had chosen a desk that she was there in the same class. Lost in his forest of hypotheticals and improbables and baseless wishing, Chon had missed an opportunity to sit next to Araceli, who was four rows of desks away.

Could he get up and move near to her? Of course he couldn't. She was too far away. So he sat watching her. She didn't look up at anyone filing in. She was done catching up with kids she'd known her whole life. There was nothing that they did this summer that was any different from what they did any other summer—except for having buried their false idols. But they didn't seem done with cozying back up to her. Chon knew they wanted to hear Araceli's stories of loss and pain, of her world being totally different and unbearable. They wanted front row seats to the breakdown.

Or maybe it was more than that. Maybe they were all like Chon. Maybe they all felt the desire to do something after a summer of hopelessness. Whatever the reason, they all sat staring at Araceli like she was some miracle they'd read about in the Bible but could never have imagined to be so wonderful and terrible and real.

Then Henry walked in. He looked at Araceli like she was his older cousin (by two weeks) and over at Chon and smiled. It was going to be a fun semester. He took the seat by Araceli and called Chon over to join them.

Chon sat behind Henry.

"Oh my god," Henry said. "Is it May yet? Shoot me in the face. Nine more months of this bullshit?"

"It'll get you ready for the world, Henry." Henry had addressed both Chon and Araceli with his complaining, so now Chon addressed them back. "You can pad your GPA with electives and your resume with extra-curricular activities so you can get into college and get a good job and never have to come back to Greenton."

There was something about talking to Henry that always made Chon mask with sarcasm what he thought or felt.

"Shit, maybe for you two assholes. My dad's already looking at buying a new truck, a four-door dooly with running lights on the roof and a brush guard on the grille. So now he can fit me, him, and her fatass father in the same truck." Henry pointed at Araceli, who smiled—because Henry and his father were both fatasses too.

The Monsevais brothers, Saul and David, worked as welders, serving the ranches around Greenton in mending gates, fences, chutes, and car parts as well as making barbecue pits and sheds and pens or anything else out of metal. Henry had been around it most of his life. When his mother died, he would accompany his father and uncle to jobs during the summers. He spent his last summer as a helper/apprentice, taking his uncle's place in his father's pickup truck because his uncle was often too hung over and despondent to face a day of work—getting to know intimately, no longer just as a spectator, the tanks and valves and hoses and motors that occupied the truck's flat bed, eating meat grilled in the small pit on the back of the rig or sandwiches heated toasty with the torch.

"They're going to move the rig onto the new truck and have a Tres Reyes logo printed on the doors. So I guess it's good that I'm here because it means a few more months before I have to ride around in that truck and become an old bastard like our dads, listening to shitty music and living out of a truck for twelve hours a day."

"You don't have to do that," Araceli said.

Henry flashed eyes at Araceli that anyone could read as saying *yeah right*, but there was something else in the look that Chon couldn't read but understood to be a Monsevais-ism.

"Well, you can always go back to school when you've made all your plata and have other people do the welding for you," Chon said.

Henry and Araceli both gave him the same look of surprise, each expressing the slightest annoyance at Chon's interloping. He barreled past them.

"But whatever. You're here on vacation. Just do all your work, cause if you don't you'll spend all your time making jokes and slowing the rest of us down."

The natural order of Chon and Henry was restored when Henry gave a *pshh* and said, "I've been carrying your fucking ass all through high school. Good luck without me in college, bitch." Mrs. Salinas walked into the room.

"Good afternoon, ladies and gentlemen," she said, loud like a kindergarten teacher. Almost too loud. "This is the second to last period of the day. You've survived most of the first day of school. I congratulate you, but I also ask that you do your very best not to fall asleep. I know that many of you have spent the entire summer waking up at around this time. It is approximately one o'clock. You are only three hours away from a nap, some of you even just an hour and a half. Be strong."

Her speech done, she looked over the students in class. The fourteen young faces in front of her made up the last fifth of the class of 1999.

"I must tell you, like I told the rest of my classes, that I am sorry for the state I was in this morning. Like I said then, it's been a hard summer. But we're all here right now and we can move on together. I'm here to talk to you and help you if you need it, just like I know all of you are here for me. In this town and in this school, we're all one big family. And that's what families do." She shut her eyes for a minute to collect herself.

Chon felt like he was watching a drunk uncle rambling because he forgot the next word he'd planned to say and couldn't remember the last one he'd slurred. He hated being forced to sit there. Mrs. Salinas was reckless like a fool, with all the self-righteous earnestness of a person who thinks they need to teach you something.

Chon looked over at Araceli. To anyone else who might have seen her, she was just another seventeen-year-old kid trying her best to ignore the horrors of a nervous breakdown as they unfolded in front of her. But Chon's eye was trained in the many faces of Araceli Monsevais. He could detect something just beneath the surface— Araceli upset, hurting, but trying to be strong. She was looking directly at Mrs. Salinas, trying to flag her down with her eyes.

Mrs. Salinas ran her fingers through the coal and silver curls that framed her face, and dragged them back across her head. When she opened her eyes again, Araceli caught them.

Chon watched the women interact. Araceli smiled warmly and patiently at Mrs. Salinas like she was saying it was all okay, like she was hurting too, like she was giving this lady almost thirty years her senior permission to feel this bad and, eventually, to feel better. Mrs. Salinas closed her eyes again and a pained smile came over her face. She shook her head in agreement, seemingly with herself. She opened her eyes and clapped her hands.

She was a new person. Or at least she was ready to try to be one.

"Alright. While I know very well, from having spoken with your previous teachers, what great students you are, I feel it's important to gauge just how much of your brilliance and skills you've retained over the summer and how much you've lost to hours of Nintendo, MTV, and stealing your parents' beers from the fridge. I'm looking at you, Monsevais," she said.

Everyone looked at Araceli, still hungry for something tragic or scandalous.

Without missing a comedic beat, Henry spoke up, "Whoa, have you and my dad already had your first parent/teacher conference or what?"

The class laughed, Araceli the loudest and most fully of them all. She looked over at her cousin. "I know he's single, Miss, but you're a happily married woman."

More laughter. Araceli gave her desk the slightest of slaps. She looked at her classmates, sharing in their laughter. When she looked at Chon, she saw that he wasn't laughing, just staring at her.

Whether or not she would ever tell him she'd noticed, Chon had been caught staring by Araceli many times in the last three years. Sometimes, on rare occasions when either she was alone or Mejia was acting like a particularly distinguished prize asshole, Chon would hold her gaze and try to speak volumes with a few seconds of shared eye contact—letting her know that he was there for her, to love her and to worship her and to never leave her alone for as long as he lived. Most times, he would look away, ashamed of his inaction and insignificance. Whichever was the case, Araceli was always merciful enough not to mention it.

This time, however, he didn't look away. He wasn't ashamed of anything, because he was looking at her in no more lustful a way than he would have looked at Mrs. Salinas. She seemed to feel found out, so Chon just smiled at her and looked at the somewhat rejuvenated teacher in front of the class.

"Henry, Henry, Henry...I've been warned about you by every teacher in the Greenton school district. I'm not really inclined to disbelieve so many wonderful teachers, but I sincerely do not think you are as dumb as you look." The class howled when she said this.

Unfazed and seemingly amused at the sparring session, Henry said, "Well, appearances are mostly deceiving, but sometimes they're regular George Washingtons. But that doesn't mean anything. For all you know, I'm lying."

Walking from her desk with a stack of tests, she said, "Yeah, they told me you'd do that too."

The test took up the rest of the hour and a half class period. Chon had forgotten the meanings of the words 'resplendent,' 'ursine,' and 'onus,' but felt he did mostly all right.

He had meant to follow Araceli to her next class, but got caught up talking to Henry about their plans for Friday night which revolved around the first game of the football season, which also revolved around staring at Araceli leading a bunch of insipid (one of the words on the test) cheers and doing back flips and cartwheels in her sexy cheerleading outfit while Chon tried his best to figure out what the hell was going on in the game.

There was no time to walk back to the cafeteria to try to see Araceli at practice. Chon had to get to work, and so he would also not be able to attend the unveiling of the framed baseball jerseys that would forever hang on the wall outside of the front office—welcoming any visitors to the school by bringing up a painful uncomfortable memory.

But he wasn't worried. Going to high school, Chon had learned over the last three years, was like living in Greenton—once you know where everyone is going to be at any given time of day, they would be there forever, like animatronic animals at an amusement park standing at the ready for their next performance to a group of children who believe they're actually living, breathing beings with the free will to step off their tracks and quit their dancing bear show to start a new life where no one throws popcorn at them and everyone they meet doesn't expect a performance and is willing to leave them in peace.

The Pachanga was empty when Chon arrived. He was scheduled to work at 2:30, but his last class didn't let out until 2:23. Most days, Chon could get to work during the passing period. On days like today, when he was caught up talking to Henry or to a teacher or following Araceli around school, Chon would have to put up with Rocha yelling curses in undecipherable Spanglish or smartass remarks from Ana.

"Chones, you're late!" she said in a cheery voice. "So what, did you fuck her? Did you take her into a stall in the boys' room and put your dick in her without even locking the latch? Did you make her beg for your little Chon-Chon?" She pinched Chon's cheek and gave it a playful slap.

"Jesus Christ, Ana. Do you have to be so damn dirty all the time?" he asked, rubbing his face like the hand she slapped him with was dirty. He looked at the counter and saw grayish-black liquid latex shavings, enough to have covered at least a dozen lottery tickets. He pointed to them.

"How many did you scratch off?" he asked her.

"Only a few, " she said, looking away like she always did when Chon asked her questions she didn't really want to answer.

"How deep in are you?"

"Just twenty dollars. You know I only ever do twenty dollars," she said, and walked back to the fountain area to fill her faded Styrofoam cup before she left.

Chon couldn't see her over the rows of groceries so he shouted into the void, "Twenty dollars on payday, Ana. You said you'd only ever do this on payday."

"Yeah, well, I got bored." She was about to say more when she saw someone pull up to Pump #1 outside. She looked at Chon and smiled. Chon tried not to seem too interested in the outcome of the transaction that was about to happen. A man got out of his car, not from in town, and stretched. He opened the cover to his gas tank and pulled the pump off the hook to put it in. Chon thought for sure the guy was going to pay at the pump. When he started walking inside without doing so, Ana gave a loud "Ha!"

"That doesn't mean anything, Ana," Chon said, not believing what he was saying. For whatever reason, whenever people paid cash for gas, they always got twenty dollars worth.

The man walked in, gave Ana and Chon, both behind the register now, a nod, and slapped a crisp twenty down on the counter.

"Pump #1, please," he said.

Ana couldn't help but laugh. When the man looked at her, eyebrow raised, she said, "I just won a bet."

The man shook his head, but left smiling when he got the feeling it wasn't him but the skinny kid behind the register who was being laughed at. Chon looked at Ana, who held her hand out, palm up.

"So, what?" Chon asked. "You're going to try to break every single rule this store has?"

"There's no rules about this," Ana said. "None at all. Now you better hurry up because that man wants to pump his gas and get the hell out of here."

She pulled her worn Discover card out of her back pocket.

"Twenty on Pump #1," she said.

Chon rang up the transaction and swiped Ana's card. He handed her the bill. When she put it in her pocket, Chon pointed to the register and said, "Your tickets?"

Ana hesitated before giving the bill back to Chon, who rang up twenty dollars' worth of lottery tickets and slipped it into the till. He had only once tried scratching off unpaid lottery tickets, and when he did it was because Ana had all but forced him after she told him about what she thought was an innocuous little scam. Sure, there were times when she would win a dollar or five or ten, but she always let it ride and always ended up owing the store money. Her illegal little slot machine for the bored never paid out. Chon couldn't stand the prospect of losing money like that on the tickets. Until that day, Chon only thought she did it twice a month.

"So wait, you're not getting off that easy," Ana said, seemingly pleased with the way the shift change was working out. "You've been waiting all summer to see this girl. You've been waiting ever since you sprouted your first little huevo curly to fuck her. Tell me, I'm asking as a friend, did you at least get to sniff her panties?"

"She's just had the worst summer of her life, and you're talking about her like that?" Chon said.

"Oh, so you talked to her about it? She told you everything? Did she lay her head on your lap and tell you about all of her bad dreams while you caressed her head? I bet you didn't say one word to her—not one word," she said.

Chon opened the register drawer for the third time to see what money he would need to drop from the safe so he had enough change to make the thirteen transactions that constituted the evening 'rush.' When Ana leaned over to grab her purse from under the counter at his feet, he moved away defensively—like he was afraid she would attack him right there, just jump his bones right in the middle of the day. She smiled and laughed at him, but Chon could tell he'd offended her.

"Just drop it, okay?" he said, checking the cigarette shelves so that he could have a reason to give her his back. He opened a carton of Marlboro reds and put them on their dispenser track.

"So, not one word? Not a hello or a goodbye. Not even, 'Please have my babies, girl of my dreams'? She really makes you some kind of pussy, doesn't she? What happened to my Chones? What happened to the skinny little beast who used to fuck my brains out and who would grunt when he came? You weren't no little bitch then."

Chon should have expected it. He probably could have even approximated the words she would say to him if he wasn't so busy wishing she wouldn't say them. This was Ana's modus operandi. If Chon, or anyone, ever said anything to hurt or offend her, she would attack with all of the venom she could muster. He figured that this came from a lifetime of living like she did—with abusive parents and husbands—and looking like she did—with legs that could never grow to match the rest of her forever-big body. He understood that it was a defense mechanism honed over years of feeling ugly, because he'd been working on his own for most of his life. But that never made the things she said hurt him any less or made him feel any better about having pushed her to hurt him in the first place.

Chon couldn't defend himself. He had no words. Ana seemed content with her shot having hit its mark and with the fact that she had regained power in the world of Ana and Chon. So she spoke up.

"You know, you have to have the absolute worst name in all of the Spanish language. I mean, I've met people named Abejundio and Venceslao and Pantaleón, but Concepcion has to be the absolute worst name for anyone to ever get—boy or girl." She looked at Chon and waited for him to acknowledge her.

When he noticed this, he said, "Yeah, I know."

"Well, yeah, you probably do. It's your shitty name. But it just hit me. I mean, to begin with, your name means fucking," she said.

"It comes from the immaculate conception," Chon said.

"Shut the fuck up." She waved his interruption away like it was a bunch of flies buzzing in front of her. "There's nothing immaculate about your name. It means fucking. Or at least getting and being fucked. Why do you think people call sex chon-chon. Can you believe I never thought of that?" The thing was, Chon hadn't either.

"And underwear? Why do you think they call them chones? And for women, you call them Concha, right? Well that means cunt." Howling with laughter, Ana started for the door. When she got there, she stopped before leaving.

"No wonder you can't talk to this little bitch. You're fucked." She walked out. As the door swung shut behind her, she shouted, "See you tomorrow, Chones!"

Chon wanted to hate Ana or even to be angry with her, but he couldn't. He was left feeling, like he always was, that what had just happened between them was all his fault. Not because he jumped back from her being in close proximity to his crotch, but because of his ever having let her blow him in the store and ever having gone to her messy, lonely house to have sex with her in a way that explored sex for the sake of anything other than to be with her, for her. He was certain he would never stop feeling bad about having been with her.

He was, however, about to rationalize by telling himself he was just a kid and she was a grown woman looking for fun too when the bell above the door rang and stole his attention—leaving him not remembering what he had been thinking about before the transaction and feeling bad for the rest of the night.

High school football is a religion in Texas, some people say—a way of life, a source of meaning in an otherwise vacuous wasteland of twenty-gallon hats and Colt revolvers. In a town whose football team actually wins more than half of their games and is in contention for post-season play, this might be the case. In Greenton, though, football was just something to do on Friday nights. If high school football really were a religion in Texas, most Greentonites would have considered themselves lapsed in their practice, if not in their very faith—why dedicate yourself to a team that would lose every Friday when there were the Cowboys to live and die for on Sunday?

But in their time as Fightin' Bitin' Greyhounds, the Johns served as the second coming of high school football in Greenton. For each of those four years, the Greyhounds made it a game or two into the playoffs—though never going beyond area play. That didn't matter, however, as it was the Johns and the thrill of their obvious supernatural abilities and shared connection on the field that the people of town were coming to see. Everyone expected the Johns to take Greenton to a state football title, but no one blamed them for not being able to. There's only so much two boys can be expected to do with nine very pedestrian, very terrestrial boys on their team and a baseball coach given a whistle and a clipboard by default.

For those four years, Greenton football was exciting. The previous collective attitude conveyed in down-turned glances that said, "Let's see how badly our boys do tonight," became, during the reign of the Johns, "Hey, these boys ain't so bad," and eventually turned to, "I think they can really do it this year!" So much can be said with a nod and a wave between neighbors when each party knows that they've lived 87% of the same life as the other.

Greenton's short-lived football excitement died before the Johns did, though. It happened halfway through the fourth quarter of the regional playoff game against the Cowboys of Premont High School when, the Greyhounds only down ten points, John Mejia was left with no open receivers (Premont's defensive coordinator dropped eight defenders into pass coverage when Robison lined up as a slot receiver) so he made a run for it on a fourth and long situation. He was met by a gang of tacklers who stopped him short of his mark, signaling a turnover on downs and the end of the Greyhounds' season and the Johns' football careers.

"Oh well," the Greentonites' shared gazes said to one another, "there's always baseball."

Football didn't just serve to distract Greentonites from their collective longing for baseball season. It was also a marker of time and progress. Football season signaled that another year had passed, forcing people to ask if it could really have been that long since they played or watched or cheered for the Greyhounds. It was also one of Greenton's only town-wide rites of passage. The first day of football season was like a new birthday, each year carrying with it a specific significance and a new set of freedoms and self-definitions.

This year the boy starts pee-wee, and the girl gets her first pair of pom-poms. This year he plays for the junior high, learning the game beyond running in a pack toward the ball from one end of the field to another. She learns choreographed dances and the joy of wearing her uniform to school on game days. Then when a kid reaches high school, there's the assumption of a role that extends beyond the football field. Boys either can't hack or don't care about football. They choose band or the break-through club or, horror of horrors, the cheer squad. And girls are either not athletic or pretty or popular or—more often the case in a small town—confident enough to join the cheer squad or drill team. There is a silent acquiescence inherent in taking on one of these other roles. The kid tells his or herself that they are not what they thought they would be, that high school isn't what they had hoped it would be, that this is how it is.

Townspeople didn't take time off from work to watch the Greyhounds practice. The retirees in town didn't bother showing up either. What would people say if they showed just how much time they had to waste? Even when the Johns were helming the ship, Greentonites kept the boys on the practice field at arm's length. That realm was for them. It was something pure, not to be sullied or besmirched by the remembering-when of adults. It was a first kiss or lay. It was sneaking out of the house in the middle of the night for stupid, somewhat dangerous, mostly harmless fun. It was youth and it was missed, and it wasn't going to be spoiled by those who had the benefit of hindsight. Besides, who could really afford to take time off of work to watch boys try to perfect the intricacies of the *Power I?*

For most Greentonites, football season started on the evening of the first game of the season, when they dusted off the old green and silver shirts, hats, and jackets to wear to the field, which they swore had a different smell on this night, but which really smelled the same.

Win, lose, or draw—on this night all bled green and silver. Despite everything, the whole town harbored fantasies of state championships and of a player separating himself from the pack, showing himself to be a man among boys and becoming something larger than his role on the field, becoming larger than the whole of Greenton.

This year that fantasy was fed by the memory of the town's fallen heroes. It was almost too much to bear. It almost made people want to give up on football and on Greyhound sports completely. Almost. But nothing could stop the siren draw of Greentonites to GHS stadium—to the sights, sounds and smell of the new school year's spectacle, to a football game and to the only thing to do in a one-stoplight town.

More than an hour before kickoff, almost every working car in Greenton was parked outside the stadium. A larger percentage of the people in Greenton were parked inside the stadium. The Dodge-nasty was among the cars, and, in the stands, Chon was happier than he ever thought he could be in the GHS stadium, creating, for once, the kinds of memories that his mind would be drawn back to in his own old age when he would return and be transported by the phenomenon that is Friday nights in a small Texas town during football season.

As kickoff approached, people in the stands got antsy. Freer's football team was on the field doing pre-game stretches and warm-ups. They even ran plays on one end of the field and practiced field goals and punting on the other.

When the stadium clock ran down to 5:00, two light booms sounded—someone tapping the mic to get everyone's attention—then Principal Adame's voice came over the stadium speakers.

"Good evening, ladies and gentlemen, and welcome to the start of the 1998 football season." The crowd roared. "We convene here today a town, a community, affected by tragedy. The events that unfolded this past spring shook many of us to our core, causing us to take stock of our lives and thank God that we still have them. Though we all still hurt and will carry that hurt with us forever, we are trying our best to heal. And we are healing. With the help of our friends and neighbors, we are getting better."

And, barely without a pause, he went on. "So, without further ado, I give you my friends and my neighbors, Arn and Angie Robison."

The crowd stood up, even those on the visitors' side, and gave a huge ovation to the two people who came arm in arm out of the tunnel under the home stands. They were an odd couple. It wasn't just that she was so beautiful and he so plain. She seemed lost under the lights, startled at the sound of the crowd's applause as if she had expected to walk out into an empty stadium, while he looked determined, like a bad actor rushing to his place on stage. Arn appeared to be pulling Angie with him to the poorly painted greyhound at the center of the fifty-yard line. When they turned to face the home crowd, however, they were indiscernible as individuals. They were a single unit, two equal parts of a machine bigger and more important than them, made so by more than thirty years of living with and for no one but each other and the boy they lost.

Angie handed Arn the microphone she'd carried out with her. He took it and regarded it like a piece of foreign technology, raising his eyeglasses over his brow and squinting at it. He flipped the switch at the side of the plastic baton and began speaking. It was a short speech that he gave, most likely a predictable one giving thanks for the support and kindness of his neighbors. It probably would have moved the entire stadium—nearly two whole towns worth of people—if the words he was speaking were being transmitted from the center of the field to the stadium speakers, to be amplified and sent into the air, broadcast on the school's AM band and out into space to be heard, millennia from now, by races of alien people tuning in to see what would become of Greenton's loss and the Robisons' pain. But the microphone was off.

Everyone sat silently, waiting for someone to do something. When it became obvious that it was too late for that, that Arn had already started and couldn't be stopped, people kept quiet from embarrassment: a man full of grief had bared his soul to an entire stadium of people who couldn't hear him.

He spoke for less than a minute, enough time for him to give a few conversational nods and a sweep of his arm to signify that he was talking about "this field" or "this town" or "this whole unfair existence where I give and give my whole life only to get one boy I put all of my hopes into and when I finally do almost a full job of raising him, I have him taken from me just when it was about to start getting really good" or something like that. His final words, "thank you," were obvious, because he gave a slight bow when he said them and he and Angie raised a couple of waves to the crowd and began to walk off.

What else was there to do but cheer?

The Robisons were met at the sideline by Coach Gallegos, who gave them hugs and exchanged a few words with them. Then the Greyhounds took the field in brand new jerseys—shiny green and silver with a thirty-four and an eight above each corner of the chest, paid for with John-star money after new uniforms were bought for the baseball team and the stars continued to sell. The crowd cheered. Rapt as they were in trying to see the new jerseys, no one in the stands paid attention to the Robisons, who exited the field and left the stadium as the teams warmed up. Almost the whole town was at the game, so no one saw them as they drove home and put their packed bags in their car and left town never to return.

With John dead, the only ties that remained between the Robisons and Greenton were painful ones. All of Arn's family was gone. When Angie's parents died, so too did all of the blood family that she had in the world worth claiming and who would claim her back.

So Arn and Angie left. It was not a romantic departure. They did not stop to share a hug and a kiss after reminiscing good times gone by in the house they designed and had built with every intention of growing old together there. They just grabbed their essentials and shut the door. It wouldn't be until the next morning—when, driving by, people would see the movers loading a van—that anyone noticed the Robisons had gone for good.

The news spread quicker than you would think, even in a town like Greenton. People felt slightly betrayed but mostly embarrassed for having let the old man talk into the turned-off microphone, for having let him and his wife live and grieve in much the same manner—with them watching and doing nothing except worrying about the propriety of their response and their emotions and themselves. When they heard about the Robison's silent exit from Greenton, a new dimension would be added to the tragedy that everyone in town was remembering and experiencing. They would begin evaluating their distance from and involvement in the Johns' deaths. It would be a sobering experience for some who would realize they had just joined in the mourning because it was something to do.

Others would realize, though, how much it really did still hurt. They had lost the Johns and now the Robisons. These were the sort of awful things that happened to other people in other towns. People couldn't believe it had happened to them.

All of this would occur because an older couple decided to pick up and leave town. But it would happen tomorrow. Tonight there was cheering to be done and memories to be made. Tonight there was a football game to be lost.

Chon pushed down on the Dodge-nasty's horn before the car came to a stop in front of Henry's house. The property—a big lawn that was almost all dirt with a small, once-white ranch house in the center, fenced all around by wrought iron—was looking better than it had all summer now that the pall of David Monsevais was removed. Once Araceli and her mother returned, he stayed at home trying to act like he had his shit half together for the sake of his daughter. Then again, it seemed to Chon that all of Greenton had taken on a new luster now that Araceli was back.

Chon had been walking through the halls of GHS with a smile on his face. He had to remember to hide it from anyone who might notice. It signaled a shift in Chon towards a happiness that could only be brought about by an act almost so self-serving as to be considered criminal. He was working with the same comforting knowledge he had always armed himself with, only now it was amplified. He was thinking about the possibility of an escape, a future.

In almost three years at the Pachanga, Chon had managed to save close to $11,000 in the account his parents had set up for him at the local bank. When Chon was fifteen, Artie Alba began paying him his minimum wage earnings in cash so as to keep his hiring a minor under wraps while not paying taxes. He took the money from the till. Chon knew his situation was a rare one, so he never brought it up to Henry or Ana or even to Pito.

His parents never required him to pay for anything other than whatever recreation he sought and the gas and repairs his car needed. He had to fight them to allow him to spend his own money on his school clothes—an expense, along with food and shelter, they viewed as their responsibility. It was the way the Gonzales family did things. It was not, however, the way most Greenton families operated: a working kid had to give every cent they earned to their parents or had to work for free at a family business or had to stay at home to babysit younger brothers and sisters or—in some cases—aging grandparents.

Chon had been obediently putting his earnings in the bank, just like his parents requested. In Chon's junior year—when the Johns signed their futures away to UT, insuring that Chon would have nine months to win the love of Araceli and whisk her away to some better future in a better place (probably junior college in Laredo or Alice or Corpus Christi)—he began to make his twice monthly deposits at the bank with the pride and determination of a wrongly convicted man digging a righteous tunnel out of the big house.

He surfed the dials on the car's radio while he waited for Henry. There was nothing good on. He settled for the first music he could find that played clearly. It was a slow pop song about, as far as Chon could tell, how some girl's love is similar to various bodies of water. The voices of the boys singing were so annoyingly saccharine that Chon considered trying for another station. But he was tired and in the same bad mood he was always in on the day of a football game.

It used to be that Chon attributed his bad mood to the fact that he was going to yet another event where the Johns were in the spotlight. But the Johns were dead. No matter, he still felt as insignificant as he always had. Was he just another nobody, no different from anyone else who went unloved and unnoticed?

Chon always had these kinds of thoughts when he waited for Henry. The only friend he had in the whole world was a fat class-clown weirdo. But people knew and generally liked the fat class-clown weirdo. Maybe it was Chon who was the social dead weight in their relationship. He hated these thoughts. He hated the song on the radio. He slammed on the horn.

"Goddamn, Chon. Don't get your panties twisted in a fucking ball," Henry said as he got into the car.

Chon hadn't seen Henry exit the house. He didn't have a chance to explain his impatience or to put the blame on Henry by complaining because before Henry even settled squarely in the passenger seat, the back door opened up and Araceli slid in.

"Hope you don't mind me joining you guys," she said, brushing her hair behind her back and buckling herself in. She smiled at Chon who looked at Henry in disbelief. Henry shrugged.

"It's really not a problem," Chon said, turning back to Araceli. She rubbed her hands, like being in the car was sending shivers down her spine. Chon's insecurities didn't have time to do their work.

"N*Sync? Really?" Henry flipped through the dial on the radio.

"It's all that was on," Chon said. He put the car in gear.

"Yeah," Henry said. He found a station playing an old Selena song and left it there. "It's all that was on that you could jack off to. Fag."

"But what are you even doing here?" Chon asked Araceli, having to work hard to look at the street in front of him.

"She was going to come with us to the game, but if you're going to be an asshole about it, we can walk," Henry said.

Chon ignored this and instead continued his questioning of Araceli.

"Aren't you supposed to be—"

She cut him off. "I quit the cheer squad. I already got my elective and P.E. credits, so I didn't really have any reason to continue in the class."

"Weren't you the captain?" Chon pulled the car onto Greyhound Way.

"I've been done with cheering for a long time. If I can't do what I want my senior year, when can I do it?"

"Man, the cheer squad pretty much shit themselves over the prospect of replacing Celi as the captain," Henry said.

"Yeah," Araceli continued. "It was pretty vicious. So they don't have a captain right now. They think I'll come back, but—"

"Fuck those bitches," Henry said. He unbuckled his seatbelt and opened the door. Somehow Chon had gotten them to the stadium and parked the car safely. He couldn't stop staring at Araceli.

"Yeah," she said with a dry chuckle. "Fuck them."

They walked to the home team entrance on the far side of the stadium. Cutting through a sea of people in Freer's blue and gold T-shirts, there were already heads turning, eyes being drawn. Araceli's celebrity extended beyond the bounds of the signs that told you—as if to try and convince you to stay—*Now Leaving Greenton.* At the Greenton fan entrance, everyone in sight of Araceli turned to stare at her, to see for themselves that she was actually still there, living and as real as anyone else among them. The attention was hard for Chon to ignore, but Araceli had practice. The death of her high school sweetheart wasn't the only reason people looked at her. This, Chon decided, is what it's like to be with, or at least stand next to, a beautiful person—so much longing and jealousy from men and women, boys and girls alike, wanting to have her, so many eyes to be ignored gracefully and tactfully.

"Goddamn, where are the bathrooms?" Henry said loudly. "I have to take a mean shit."

Henry's outburst made people turn away. Conversations took a new direction, went to the jerseys that the boys would supposedly be wearing. Henry walked ahead of the people in front of him, glaring at anyone who would let him in, as if to tell them that they were the ones who had made an awkward situation of his digestive goings on.

"He's really good at that," Chon said.

"Yeah." Araceli was laughing. "I just can't tell sometimes if he's doing it for me or for his own amusement."

"Oh, I'm sure it's fifty/fifty, right down the middle." Chon looked out on the field at the Freer players warming up, trying to use the distraction as a means of not suffocating Araceli with his attention or falling all over her every word and gesture.

"But, I'll tell you, he's the only reason I've survived this place," Araceli said. "If I didn't have him to make a joke of everything here, to make fun of me when I take myself and my bullshit too seriously, I think I'd have gone crazy by now.

"You know, you grow up without any siblings and you're forced to spend all this time with your cousin and you're told, of course, that you have to love him like a brother. But I can really see why you'd be friends with him. If he loves someone like he loves you" —Chon rolled his eyes here, but Araceli waved his stupid machismo away—"like he loves me, he'll do anything to make things better for you."

They got to the front of the line. It was five bucks to get into the game.

"I don't have my money, Henry does." She looked up into the stands to see if she could spot her cousin.

"Don't worry," Chon said. "I'll get them."

He gave the kid in the ticket booth a ten and got two tickets and a look of disbelief from the guy in return. Chon guessed the kid was trying to do the math: what would put *her* there with *him* on a Friday night when there were so many other people who would be better suited to take up her time and attention. *Screw him.*

Chon watched Araceli walking slowly across the bottom of the stands. He wondered what she was thinking, if maybe she was only now realizing what she had done—quit the cheer squad and come to the first football game with two of the least popular people in school. She was just like everyone else now, a spectator, no longer a star of the whole show of Greenton football on a Friday night.

"Sorry," she said behind her shoulder, her eyes peeled in search of her cousin, her attention so focused it emanated the kind of poise she would probably need to get through this night. "I haven't had to pay for a game since, like, the seventh grade. I'll pay you back when we find Henry."

"Don't worry about it," Chon said. "I insist."

He said these last two words right when Araceli turned to look at him. They must have struck her in a funny way, because she gave him a look that seemed to say she didn't want him or anyone else buying her way anywhere. Maybe she wasn't ready for it so soon after John, maybe that's the kind of girl she was, but her reaction came out of her like a warning—*take a step back*. It stopped him cold. They would have stood there in front of rows and rows of people in green and silver, almost all watching them—her, then him by proxy—if Henry hadn't called down from the stands.

They walked up to the stretch of aluminum bench Henry had claimed for the three of them. It was very near the top row, at the far end of the stands—a seat selection made by someone who didn't care—or want—to be seen by any of the players or cheerleaders or general passers-by, someone with instincts honed over years of existing, with Chon at his side, on the periphery of anything that mattered at school or in town. How serendipitous it was that he had forged such an existence—serendipitous and useful to Araceli. He and Chon were like Greenton's two-man witness protection program.

"They were so freaked out at the idea of me shitting myself that they didn't make me pay to get in," Henry said, laughing.

"Speaking of," Araceli said. "Can I see my wallet? I need to pay Chon back for my ticket."

Pulling the wallet out of his pocket, Henry shook his head.

"What, you couldn't just pay for her, you cheap asshole? You work so many hours at that damn store and you can't spare five bucks?"

Chon looked at Henry, then at Araceli shuffling through her wallet and pulling out five singles. She straightened them out and faced them all in the same direction. Chon was certain then that he would love her forever.

"It starts with five dollars. Then she's borrowing my car and asking to copy my homework," Chon said. He took the money from Araceli and gave her a smile that told her he would keep their moment of silent understanding forever in his confidence.

"One fucking time!" Henry said. "One time I copy your homework and you act like I owe you a kidney or something."

"Don't worry, Chon, my dad lets me borrow the Suburban whenever I want to. The Dodge-nasty's safe from me. But I need a report on *Candide* by Monday," she said.

"Wait, Celi, I copied his homework once, but it was for a failing grade," Henry said. "This guy's dumber than shit."

Araceli laughed out loud. Seeing her this happy, made so by his presence, if only as the butt of a joke, Chon was lost in taking in a whole new side of Araceli—in adding these brand new perceptions to the bank of knowledge he'd once only stocked for imaginary and masturbatory purposes—so lost that he dropped the ball in the game of witty and stupid repartee. The two of stood looking at him, standing slack-jawed and unaware of the turn their conversation had taken Chon in.

"Aww," Araceli said. "C'mon, Chon. We're only playing. You don't have to sit and sulk. We'll be nice, I promise."

She grabbed his arm and gave it a little squeeze. Her thumb hit his bicep and her fingers made to reach around to his triceps, but got lost in the width of his deltoid. He melted. This was the culmination of all of his working out and preening, of his minutes and hours spent staring at himself in the mirror, assessing what could be fixed and trying to cover up what couldn't be mended.

She looked at him in a way that Chon believed meant that she saw him as a man. But he could be wrong. He could always be wrong.

"Where's the fucking team?" Henry asked. "Shouldn't they be stretching and warming up to get ready for their ass-whooping?"

"C'mon, Henry, where's your pride?" Chon said, snapping out of his reverie. "You should be bleeding green and silver like the rest of us fightin' bitin' Greyhound fans."

"Ah, bullshit. There's no way in hell we're going to win this game. This town is doomed to suck at football for all of eternity. Shit, we couldn't even win when—" Henry stopped, making no attempt at a smoothing over of this rare occasion when the bullshit he usually slung with artful irrelevance actually hit someone. He looked at Chon with a pained expression on his face, then up at the stadium lights above Freer's football supporters. Araceli looked at Henry like she was more touched by him caring about her feelings than hurt by the near-mention of her dead boyfriend.

"I guess you're right," Chon said. "If we couldn't win when the Monsevais brothers 'dominated the line on both offense and defense,' there's no hope."

"Oh my god, has my uncle told you that story?" Araceli shouted, then gave Chon a playful slap on the arm. Chon laughed.

"No, but that's what this one always says when they're at the house cracking beers and reliving the old glory days." Chon pointed at Henry with his thumb, and Henry missed a beat. But composure and expectation and the existence he'd cut out for himself won the day, and Henry got back in the game.

"'We overpowered 'em, flipped people over and smashed them in the ground,'" Henry said in the voice Chon knew to be an imitation of his drunk father. "Never mind the fact that they won three games in four years."

They all laughed. The addition of Araceli to their end-of-the-bleachers clique made Chon almost happier than being close to what he'd coveted for so long. He felt like he had friends. A group. Not just him and the other guy picked last at recess being friends by default. That's not what he and Henry actually were, but it was hard not to feel that way on a Friday night when Greenton's teenagers partied and rode around together in cars and made out and fucked and he was stuck in the Monsevais' dirty living room or, even worse, parked in the Dodge-nasty on the side of the road somewhere, drinking warm beers with the only person, outside his family, who would even realize he was missing if he disappeared.

This was the verification of something that Chon had thought to be an artificial construct of the storytellers of the generation before his—the idea of high school as the best time of their lives. Because how could that have been anything but a lie when Chon was so miserable and—as near as he could tell and despite how hard they tried to hide it—nearly everyone around him was too? But being there, at Greenton stadium on a Friday night for the opening kickoff of the season, Chon could see that there was some truth to the lies he had felt so let down and cheated by. It was in the shared laughter of Henry, Araceli, and himself. It wasn't anything more than that. Years down the line they would all forget who Greenton played that night and what the score ended up being and even what they talked about, but they would remember, if not that very instance of laughter, that they had friends. They were young, they were innocent, and, on that night, they had fun.

Chon let his thoughts drift. He realized that if the Johns were alive, he would not be where he was right now, with Araceli at his side and a smile on his face. He was grateful, in a way he could never say out loud, for things having transpired this way. It was a fleeting thought, predicated by Chon never having really felt like he did just then. He would have chastised himself in the form of a silent head shake and stuffed the ugliness back to the recesses of his subconscious where it belonged if the crowd hadn't hushed right then and Arn Robison and his wife walked out of the tunnel to take center field, to give a speech that no one could hear.

"So the poor bastard gave a speech to a stadium full of people and the microphone was off?" Ana said. "And not one person in the place bothered to help him?"

Chon shook his head.

Ana was sitting in her usual seat on the ice machine. "That's pretty fucked up, man." She took a pull off her cigarette. She closed her eyes. The smoke issued slowly out of her nostrils. It was all Chon could do not to swat the smoke away from his face.

"How've you been, Ana?" he asked. "We haven't talked in a long time."

She opened her left eye and looked down at Chon. Her eyebrow was raised like she was checking to see if this was something worth waking up for. He wanted to comfort her in some way, but how without giving her the wrong idea? How did it come to this between him and this lady? When did they begin this dance of resentment and regret? Is this verbal and emotional tightrope walking all that would ever become of relationships? Of sex? Or was it work? Was it the age difference? Was it Greenton? Chon foolishly believed that this awkwardness was brought about by the strange circumstances of his having gotten involved with Ana, that he would someday be able to answer these questions.

Something in his face made her sit up and rub the tired out of her eyes.

"I talked to you yesterday," she said. She snuffed the burning filter she held in her hand and lit a fresh cigarette. "Well, I guess I've been alright. No news to report here. Just coming into work and going home and then coming into work and going home. What is there for me to tell you? You know the ins and outs of my life. It ain't pretty, but I'm here."

Chon nodded and stood, wondering if he should speak into the awkward void of Ana's silence. Ana's voice was flat. He hadn't heard her speak in so long without a coquettish raise or malicious dip to her words that he'd forgotten what she sounded like when she was occupied with anything other than Chon and getting his attention or making him feel like shit. He didn't want to be back in the front of her mind, not necessarily. It's just that that was the Ana he'd taught himself to deal with. Sure, he'd been keeping her at arm's length. That way, he could tell how she was doing. It's not like he ever stopped caring about her.

"And Tina?" he asked.

At the mention of her daughter's name, Ana looked at Chon, sizing him up, his intentions. She was calculating his latitude and longitude on the plane of friend or foe. She let out a sigh and shook her head.

"Still up in San Antonio. I had to ask Bexar County to drop all of the charges against her father so that she could live with him. She said she'd be cool—stay clean, piss in cups, go to school, the whole deal—but only as long as she didn't have to come back and live here in Greenton. Her dad's still a fuckup, but he's trying. She's run away a few times, but there's a cop that's helping us, helping her. I think they're fucking, but not in a messed up way. He's real young, she's almost seventeen. I think he likes her."

Chon nodded.

"And things are seeming like they might be better. We're talking on the phone almost every day. Chones, I'm about as happy with the way things are going as I was before she hit puberty and turned wild and got caught with that Marquez fucker and left me alone here in this shithole. What's getting me is this: before it was almost like I didn't have a daughter, just a ball of problems that I didn't really have to deal with because she was there and I was here. But now I talk to her, and I'm getting to know her, and she's really smart and funny, and I'm hurting because I'm not with her. Is that fucked up?—that it almost hurts more now that she's doing okay without me?"

Chon stood there, listening, finally over himself and his (non)involvement in the sad state of Ana's being. Tears started rolling slowly down her face. They traced a slick outline of it, of Ana. Face framed as it was in the glow of the westward-leaning sun behind Chon, Ana looked like a different person.

Chon put his hand on her knee. She grabbed it and held it, crying through closed eyes and still bringing her cigarette to her lips with her other hand. She gave Chon's hand a final squeeze and let go.

"And you?" she said, wiping away the tears on her face with her sleeves. "You getting anywhere with your chula?"

"You know what, I am. But it's nothing worth mentioning right now. I'll let you know when something real happens."

Ana made to slide off of the cooler. Chon gave her his hand to help her down.

"Sounds like you're saying nothing's happening," Ana said. "You don't have to lie to make yourself look cool, because I know you aren't."

Chon laughed.

"Really, it's kind of happening. I just don't want to jinx it." He opened the door for her.

"I get that," Ana said. She walked to the register and closed her till. She was out of the store in less than ten minutes, leaving Chon with little more than goodbye and forty-five minutes to himself until the next customer came in.

★

The following Saturday night, Chon was still there. There again, really, but the predictability of it all created a dependable, if not suffocating, state of static flux. He could move, live, study, work with his eyes closed and at any given time know where he was and what he was supposed to be doing. Life was a series of reruns of a not too interesting show when nothing else was on. This was especially the case at work now that Araceli had joined him and Henry in their regularly scheduled daytime programming.

Chon's plans to win her had been circumvented by the actuality of her existing in his day-to-day life, live and in person. It was so much easier to seduce the objectified idea of someone than to actually listen to and enjoy spending time with that same person.

He stood at the register, counting down the minutes of his last hour at work more intently than on any other Saturday night. Tonight was GHS's homecoming dance. At that minute, Araceli would be crowned homecoming queen, looked on and talked about by a whole gym full of students whose compassion had died and who were back to envying and lusting after her. Chon had decided that he would close the store an hour early—at eleven, when the dance would be ending—so that he could run home, shower, and dress for the party Araceli had invited Chon and Henry to—Chon and Henry who weren't invited to parties unless they were providing the spirits.

By ten-thirty, Chon had the store swept and mopped and the cooler, condiment trays and cigarette racks stocked. After every customer who came in, Chon restocked whatever they had bought. The store looked better than it had in a long time. If Sammy or Artie Alba had anything to say about the fact that Chon shut down early, he would point to the fact that while he didn't put in his whole eight hours, the seven he did put in were better than anyone else's. Chon was thinking about the possibility of getting caught. He came to the same conclusion that set his mind at ease every time he sold a case of beer to an underage friend or rang up and charged nineteen loaves of bread to someone's Lone Star card in exchange for a carton of smokes: he was a good employee.

10:37. Chon was still lost in thinking about getting caught, fired, maybe even ticketed or arrested for all of the times he sold to minors and defrauded the state's welfare system—all worth it. Like the party at the Saenz ranch that last spring, selling three whole kegs and letting the ice cooler be almost emptied by classmates who didn't like or care about him. But it was worth it because he was seen as someone other than an insignificant loser. Or so he thought. And Araceli saw him. And smiled and gave him a little half wave from her tailgate throne at the side of the person who, at the time, Chon had sworn to be his chief enemy.

Today there was no enemy. Today it would not be just a smile and a little half wave. A year ago, Chon would have burned the Pachanga to the ground for the chance to have the kind of interaction he would have with her tonight.

10:40. The warm halogen glow of an SUV's headlights pushed its way through the cold, white fluorescence of the Pachanga's storefront, waking Chon up and making him thankful for a distraction, however small, from the slow turning of time during the last, and longest, minutes of his workday. He grabbed a squirt bottle of all-purpose cleaner and a rag and began cleaning the counter in front of him for want of something to do with his hands. The bell above the door rang. Chon looked up. It was Henry—shirt and tie, pressed slacks, shined two-tone Stacy knockoffs, hair actually combed—looking clean. And Araceli in a T-shirt, warm-ups, an old pair of cross-trainers.

"Gimme all the money in the register and no one has to get hurt," Henry said, thumb and forefinger gun raised, pointing at Chon's face.

"Any of you fucking pricks move, and I'll execute every last one of ya!" Araceli shouted in a funny voice like she was quoting someone. Chon and Henry looked at her quizzically.

"It's from a movie," she said. "We'll have to watch it sometime."

"What are you guys doing here? The dance isn't even over," Chon said.

"Oh my god, if I had to sit through another goddamn Shania Twain song, I was going to kill someone," Henry said. He walked back to the cooler and grabbed an eighteen-pack of beer.

"Did you win?" Chon asked Araceli.

"Yeah," she said. She was in house clothes, comfortable as could be, but her hair was still done up in curls with a couple of strands falling down on either side of her face. Her makeup made her look like a pageant contestant.

"I got the crown, got the pictures for the parents, and we took off. We went to my house and I changed. We baked a couple of pizzas, but I thought we should come get you before someone ate them all."

Henry put the beer and a Snickers bar on the counter. Chon rang it up, took Henry's money, and gave him correct change all without looking away from Araceli.

"Hey," Henry said, pointing a finger at Araceli, "I'd be doing you a favor. You eat enough pizza, you'll look like me with a wig and makeup on."

Now Chon looked to Henry, eyebrow raised.

"I got you thinking about that, don't I?" Henry said, laughing. "You're picturing me as a woman right now, aren't you? Yeah, she ain't the girl of your dreams when I put it that way, now is she?"

Chon and Henry shared a look that contained multitudes—*Fuck you* and *I'm sorry* and *As soon as she's not around, I'll kick your ass.* The moment didn't have time to become awkward. Araceli intervened.

"You give yourself too much credit," she said, not letting on, in true Monsevais fashion, whether she was smoothing things over or so rapt in trying to get the next jab in that she honestly didn't catch all of the meaning in her cousin's banter. "Think about it this way: if you lost a hundred pounds and put on a dress and makeup, you'd still be dogshit ugly. I don't mind saying I'm not dogshit ugly. So if you gave me all of that made up weight you'd be losing, I'd still be winning crowns and you'd still be an asshole." They all laughed.

"You never stick up for yourself," she told Chon. "You have to punch back every now and then. So, as you might be able to tell from my clothes, we're not going to any stupid party tonight. We're just going to hang out and watch movies or something at my house. My parents are at a wedding in Laredo, won't be back till late."

"You coming?" Henry asked.

"Yeah," Chon said. "I was going to go home and change after I closed—"

"If I'm dressed like this, you can wear your work clothes," Araceli said.

10:58. Chon turned off the store's lights, locked up, and followed Araceli to her house, the house he'd driven by so many times hoping to catch a glimpse of her through a window, in the front yard, getting groceries from the car, anything. They drank until the early morning hours, not watching the TV that was on and talking about absolutely nothing that mattered. If either Sammy or Artie Alba found out that the store was closed an hour and two minutes early, they never said anything to Chon.

The weeks passed like this. Weeks, then months, with Chon working and living for the weekend. Everything revolved around the time he spent with Araceli and Henry. He felt that Araceli's presence in his life granted him a degree of normalcy he never had before, had never even striven for. She had bestowed upon Chon a life worth thinking about.

But Chon was not satisfied. He wanted more. He wanted her. He was convinced that what he felt for Araceli was real love. After all, his feelings showed that he wasn't trying to get anything from the girl but the girl herself.

Araceli's inclusion in nearly every facet of Chon's life—hanging out before school and at lunch, sitting together in class, going out on weekends—was, of course, what Chon had always wanted, but the novelty of friendship was wearing off and the reality of that friend being Araceli—up close, in the flesh, painfully beautiful—was starting to set in. After three months of close interaction with her, Chon felt sure he wasn't much closer to existing in her eyes as a romantic possibility.

It was a Friday. The Greyhounds were playing their final game of the season in Corpus Christi, the last of their high school careers. Araceli would be doing the driving that night since Chon didn't trust the Dodge-nasty to make it all the way to Corpus and neither she nor Henry cared to ride in a car without A/C, regardless of the few degrees November had made the temperature in Greenton drop. Chon went home straight from school that day—he'd requested the day off from work—shaved, showered, and ate a snack. By three o'clock, he was ready to go. He sat in the living room ignoring Pito and whatever he was watching on TV, thinking of all of the ways in which he could make some sort of progress with Araceli.

Just after four, there was a knock at the door. Chon, who was lost in his scheming and fantasizing, was surprised at the sound. He wasn't expecting anything more than a honk and the Suburban idling on the street, Henry and Araceli as eager to get on the road as any teenaged Greentonite had ever been. But it was Araceli standing alone at the door, as beautiful and perfect as she was in any dream he ever had about her.

"Bad news, Chon," Araceli said. "An eighteen-wheeler went off the road outside of Zapata. Everyone's okay, the guy just fell asleep. Thing is, they called Dos Reyes to mend the fence—after hours, emergency pay—so that they don't lose any more stock. So my dad, my uncle, and Henry all went to do their thing. There's a herd of cattle walking all over Highway 16. Crazy shit, huh?"

Chon nodded his head. He forced the words, "Yeah, crazy," out of his mouth. Disappointment was overtaking him so suddenly, he was afraid that he would shudder visibly in front of Araceli. And Pito was staring at him, ready to watch a happy Chon crack and crumble and turn to dust at the prospect of a night without the only girl in town, anywhere, he'd ever wanted to be with.

He was being rejected by Araceli. She couldn't bear the idea of being with him without Henry as a buffer. That's what he figured.

"So I guess it's just the two of us," she said. "I'll try not to bore you too much." She turned around and took the porch steps of the Gonzales house two at a time. She was halfway down the walkway when she noticed Chon wasn't on her heels.

Her hair did the funny thing, like she was some kind of model doing *pleasantly surprised* for the cameras, where it hopped perfectly over her shoulder to reveal her smiling face. She turned and called to Chon, "You coming?" He still didn't believe that he was.

In the front seat of her father's Suburban, after some forced and stunted small talk about his day at school and that evening's upcoming game, Chon finally relaxed.

He laid his head back and closed his eyes for a second. He grinned, helpless to do anything else. When he sat up and looked over at Araceli, he could see she'd been watching him.

"I bet you're happy you're not working right now," she said.

"You know what?" he replied. "I really am."

Araceli smiled and looked out at the road in front of them. On the radio, what had otherwise been ignorable acoustic singer-songwriter crooning caught Chon's ear. There was a line about lying to someone, saying they would be friends 'till the day that we die.' It was music Chon had never heard, too light to be played on the harder-leaning rock stations that came in from Corpus and Laredo, too weird to be played on the country stations, too indie sounding for MTV.

"What's this?" Chon said, pointing to the radio.

"Oh, it's this guy from Austin. His name is Bob Schneider." Chon wrinkled his chin and bobbed his head up and down in approval. "The people I stayed with last summer went to a bunch of shows at this restaurant/bar place that had fake surfboards as tables and was like a block away from the water. They always invited me to come. I didn't know them. You know? I didn't want to be there. But one night I decided to go. So I was there, all sad and mopey, and the band came on, and I just had a good time. There wasn't even really anything about the songs that spoke to me or anything like that. I think I was just ready to let myself have fun. So I bought the album and it totally surprised me. The show was energetic and funky and kind of crazy, and the album is like this. When I listened to it all the way through, I wasn't expecting it to be soft and sweet and meaningful. I cried. I listened to it over and over again. It kind of became the soundtrack of my summer."

They sat riding, everything quiet but the sound of the treads humming on the highway and Bob Schneider singing and playing his guitar. Lulled into a state of comfort so profound as to make him forget the magnitude of the situation—him, Araceli, alone together on the road, the opportunity he'd waited so long for—Chon spoke without thinking.

"So I bet you did all kinds of cool stuff this summer." He was looking out into nothing, as if trying to watch the sound waves in front of him as the music bent and bounced them. When Araceli didn't respond, Chon looked over at her.

"Well, it certainly wasn't another Greenton summer," she said, seeming hard-pressed even to have come up with that.

Chon wanted to speak, but about what? His summer? How all he did was think of ways to capitalize on the death of the Johns?

"I had a lot to deal with," she said after a while. "More than anyone knows."

"Yeah, I can only imagine what you went through."

"That's not it, though." Araceli blew her breath out like she was trying to rid her lungs of a poison. "You assume it's because of what happened with John. You assume I shut myself in a room I couldn't even lock the door to because I had to share it with some twelve-year-old girl I barely knew because John died, because him and Robison crashed their car. You think I spent every day this summer, every single day, crying because my boyfriend died. Which is sad. It tore me apart. But there were things you don't know, things no one knows."

Chon could have done two things just then. He could have looked away from Araceli and stared at the fence posts they were passing and the thickets of brush and cactus and bare mesquite trees that were cutting chaos on the horizon as the setting sun glowed weakly behind them. He could have let her cry her silent tears so he could compartmentalize what she was going through, classify it as something to swallow and hide. It would have been the easy thing to do, but it wasn't what he actually did.

He sat up in his warmed captain's chair, ran his hands through his hair, reached over into the void that separated him from all he'd ever wanted, his hand stopping roughly halfway between the two of them to turn off the radio.

"Like what, Araceli? What don't I know?"

She shook her head. Sobs pulled her chest in. Her shoulders seemed to be trying to touch one another. Chon adjusted his seat belt and turned in his seat to face her full-on. "You can tell me," he said.

Araceli looked over at Chon. When their eyes met, she cried harder, almost crazy-like. A whine began to accompany her sniffles, a long, deep whine—all chest and pain. She looked back to the road. Chon figured that maybe, from the way she looked at him, Araceli would share her burden as soon as she stopped crying. He waited.

The game's byline was as bad as it could have been expected to be. The Greyhounds lost to the Bears 57-13. It was a brutal ending to a brutal season. What was unexpected was the way the game started. The Greyhounds won the coin toss. But Coach Gallegos deferred possession of the ball—like he did every time the team won a toss, insisting it showed strength and instilled confidence in his team when, really, all is did was allow a team to ram right through the porous Greyhound defense on the way to a blowout. The Bears returner juked and hurdled his way down to the Greenton thirty-five-yard line when one of his blockers threw a hit so hard on the scrawny fútbolero-come-kicker that the poor kid flew back a good five feet, directly into the would-be scoring path of the runner. His helmet hit and dislodged the ball from the runner's hand. Greenton possession.

"He broke up with me," she told him. "Right there, in front of almost everybody in town.

I knew it was coming. But I was more upset about him breaking up in front of everyone than I was about the actual break-up."

The Greyhounds scored a touchdown on what was not so much a trick play as a botched one—a Statue of Liberty-type thing that no one at the game could fully describe in terms any more technical than crazy, miraculous, and badass. Then there was the legitimate defensive stand on the next series that had the Bears going three and out. This resulted in good field position that made possible a forty-four yard field goal, compliments of the battered but back-patted and ass-slapped kicker given credit for, and made confident by, his 'play' on the ball that resulted in Greenton's touchdown drive.

"Oh my god," Chon responded. "He broke up with you. You had to deal with getting dumped and then with the fact that the guy who did it died? I'm sorry, Celi." Chon had never used the diminutive of her name—something reserved for her family members and probably John Mejia. It had just come off his tongue then, but she didn't so much as raise an eyebrow at his familiarity. "I'm so sorry."

With the 10-0 lead, Greenton's fans were heartened, excited even. They hadn't learned the lessons of weeks and years gone by. Of course the Bears, physically superior and already playoff-bound, came back. Their running back—who was voted All-State and had won a scholarship to Baylor that he never cashed in on account of a simple breaking-and-entering that turned to accessory to homicide when the homeowner died from blows to the head that resulted from the struggle he had with the athlete's accomplice—ran for five touchdowns and almost five hundred yards. With every Bear score and Greyhound turnover or dropped pass, Greenton's fans lost a little bit of hope. By the end of the game, they were more dejected than they would have been had the boys lost by 100 touchdowns. They filed out of the stands, walked out to their cars and probably drove all the way home in silence.

"That's not it," she told him. "That was bad enough, but no one knew we had broken up when he died. So his mom thought we were still together. She feels this connection with me—like he was ours. She called me every day this summer. Every day. She came over to the house the day after I got back and just went crazy. She was bawling and screaming. Then it was like I lost him all over again, like I left town to hide from something and as soon as I got back I was forced to deal with it."

Chon had bitten on the bait of the last game of his high school career ending with a win like everyone else around him. He believed they could do it, that they were going to. He didn't take the loss as hard as everyone around him, as hard as Araceli did. When the Bears took the lead, 14-10 before the end of the first quarter, he knew it was all over. But he cheered and yelled just like everyone else. He grimaced and groaned with his neighbors at the down-by-down developments of the massacre. He was hoarse and tired by the end of the game.

"I couldn't tell her that he had broken up with me. The truth wasn't worth adding another layer of bullshit for her to deal with. But she kept on calling to talk to me about what she was going through and what she thought I was going through. It has gotten to the point where I go over to see her every other day or so. She just stays home, not leaving the house even for work. My visits are the only reason she gets dressed and does herself up."

Araceli pulled into the stadium parking lot when she finished her confession. She looked at Chon, her face pinched up, waiting for what he would say.

"And you still haven't told her?" Chon had asked.

Araceli shook her head. "I can't."

"Stupid question, huh?

Araceli took off her seatbelt and opened her door, hesitating. Would she add more? Chon looked at her, but she got out of the Suburban and slammed the door behind her.

After the game, Chon and Araceli grabbed a couple of burgers to go. Araceli insisted since Chon had to open the Pachanga in the morning. Chon sorted the food, propping Araceli's French fry box in the cup holder nearest her and re-wrapping her burger so she could eat it one-handed without getting dirty. He handed her the burger and asked if she wanted ketchup. When he did, Araceli looking at him sideways and smiled. He blushed, thankful she couldn't see him in the dark.

"Can you believe that game?" Araceli asked.

"Yeah," Chon said. "They killed us."

"But that first quarter. I thought we were could actually win. I thought our last game would be a win."

"Yeah, me too." Chon took a bite of his burger and turned the radio back on to cover the sounds of his chewing.

"I could tell. I think that's the only time I've heard you cheer all season." Araceli pointed a fry at Chon. "You're almost as much of an asshole as my cousin."

Mouth full, Chon couldn't retort. Araceli laughed.

"You know, I think I'm actually going to miss this. Games, road trips, yelling for a horrible team, all of it. Not even because I like it, but because it's all I know. For the first time all season, I wished I could be down on the sidelines cheering with the girls. I wanted to have it back for five minutes—just one cheer or dance routine—and then go back up to the stands with you. But you can't have it that way, can you? I think that's what it's going to be like after graduation. We're going to leave home and wish for just a little we could be back here. "

"I never thought I would ever wish for any of my time in high school," Chon said. He drank from his soda to clear his mouth. "To tell the truth, I've hated most of it. It wasn't so horrible, but I've felt like a no one, like Henry was the only person who knew I existed."

"So you need people to know you exist? You need to be seen?"

"No," Chon paused here, unsure of what to say, then unsure if he should say it. "But I wanted to feel like someone cared about me."

Araceli looked over at Chon. The very fact of their sharing space in the car at that moment made him look away. Her looking at him right then made him want to jump out. She took a last bite of her burger, put what was left neatly on the center console and, with a wipe of her hand on her jeans, grabbed the steering wheel at ten and two and stared out at the road.

They approached the bright white pump lights of a gas station that signaled Driscoll, Texas ahead of them. There were still two hours of dark, mostly middle-of-nowhere driving, ahead of them. Araceli pulled the Suburban into the station and up to a pump. She did a thing Chon had been noticing of late. She leaned her head slightly to the right to crack her neck, her shoulders rising up and rolling back, and her hands rising to her yawning face—always that sequence, always in one fluid motion like she was summoning something up from deep inside of her and expelling it with a pleasure as simple as waking up from a satisfying nap.

It was here that Araceli walked a fine line between beautiful and sexy, someone he wanted to love and someone he wanted. It killed him. It always had, all of the wanting and longing to no avail. But now, the new dimensions of his actual earned, interactive knowledge made it more exhilarating than torturous. Araceli's neck pop-back stretch-yawn move woke Chon to the fact that while he was riding back home from a game, baring his soul and making embarrassing confessions to a new friend, that was not all he was doing. He was doing it all with the girl he'd thought about constantly for as long as he cared to remember, and that was larger than the sum of its mundane parts. He was sitting in a car with Araceli, the girl he had lost and the woman he had since declared to himself to be the most everything anywhere. The good life was spending an evening alone with the girl of your dreams, and Chon was living it.

"Are we on empty?" he asked.

"No, but we should fill up to be safe."

"Alright, I'll get it." Chon unbuckled his seatbelt and opened the door to go in and pay for gas.

"Stop it," Araceli said, loud but not angry.

"What?"

"You paid for the tickets to the game and then you paid for the burgers. Stop it. I'll pay for the gas." Araceli got out of the Suburban and started for the store. Chon followed her. "I'm not going to let you pay, so don't even try."

"Fine," he told her. "I just thought I'd walk into the store with you. Keep you company."

Araceli gave the cashier a twenty. The guy didn't bother to put down the phone to make eye contact when he whispered *thanks*. Chon hated gas station service like that. Worse, he hated more the fact that it was something he noticed.

Araceli walked quickly to the pump, as if she were racing Chon. She took the handle off the hook and put it in the Suburban's gas tank.

Seeing that she was having some difficulty, Chon offered silently to help. Araceli grimaced at his gesture, but he insisted by grabbing the handle, squeezing it, and thumbing down the lever that rigged it to pump on its own.

"Don't mean to step on your toes. I'm good with these things, kind of my job," Chon said.

They stood there, listening to the sound of trucks idling at the station and trucks passing by on the highway, to the rush of gasoline flowing through hoses into the Suburban. Chon grabbed a squeegee from a bucket next to the pump. He went to work ridding the Suburban's windshield of dead bug parts. He did it in a few quick motions, and had the squeegee back in the bucket by the time Araceli's twenty dollars' worth of gas was done pumping. When it was, Chon put the handle on the hook and opened the driver's door for Araceli. He made a gesture like a chauffeur.

"Thank you for your business today. Be safe in your travels and come back and see us if ever you're down Greenton-way," he said in faux-broadcast voice. "I mean, Driscoll-way," he corrected himself, speaking normally.

Araceli didn't move. She had been watching Chon's gas station attendant routine, arms crossed and lips uncurved in neither smile nor frown.

She pointed the ignition key at Chon and said "Listen," in such a tone that Chon didn't know what to expect her to say next. "I'm not being bitchy or cold. I just get tired of guys always trying to pay or to treat or to step in and fix something that's not broken or help me with something I can do on my own. John did it all the time. It pissed me off no end. I just wanted to let you know that. So I did."

She was dead serious. She stood there, arms crossed, left hand in the crook of her right elbow, right hand extended to Chon with a truck key claw as a pointer—like she was going to fight him using the Praying Mantis kung-fu technique—her face not really scowling, though it might as well have been for as unused to seeing Araceli unsmiling as Chon was.

"So I won't pay for you," Chon said, cautiously. "And I'm sorry about pumping the gas."

"Well, it's your job," Araceli said. "I'd give you a tip, but I just used all of my cash for gas."

"Don't worry," Chon said. "I'll pay the tip...wait, never mind."

Araceli laughed and threw the keys at Chon. When they bounced off of his chest, she laughed harder. Chon bent down to pick up the keys and rubbed his chest where they had hit him.

"So now you become violent with me?"

She walked away from Chon around the back of the Suburban.

"I was hoping you'd drive," she told him. "I'm feeling kind of tired."

"No problem," he told her. "Just don't hit me with anything while I'm driving."

They got in the Suburban and buckled up. Chon adjusted the driver's seat to accommodate his long legs, and Araceli turned down the radio and leaned her seat back to roughly the same angle as a dentist's chair. She closed her eyes.

Chon put the car in gear and turned onto F.M. 665 towards Alice. They crossed over Highway 77. Araceli spoke without sitting up in her seat.

"They came through here, John and Robe. They drove up 77 when they left—when they died." She stopped here, seeming to be listening back to the word she'd just said—like she had never said it, not just about the Johns, but in her life, like she was learning a new word in a language foreign to her ears and tongue. "They drove up to Highway

181, where they died." She said it differently this time, like she had just learned the word and wanted to use it as much as she could so as to not forget its pronunciation.

"Why?" Chon said. "Why would they come over to 77 when they could have taken 16?"

Araceli made a quarter turn away from Chon and curled her legs up. Chon looked over at the ball she'd made of herself and wondered if she was turning toward sleep or away from his question.

"We don't know," she said, not moving to face him. "They didn't tell anyone that they were coming this way, they always did that. But where they died, off of 181, I think they were visiting a girl John had told me about. He said she lived in Sinton."

"A girl?" Chon asked.

"Yeah," Araceli said so quiet that Chon almost didn't hear her. "He had told me about a girl he'd met, from Sinton. He said she didn't mean anything and just happened to mention in passing that she was from there. It's probably nothing, but that's where they ended up dead—just north of there."

She stopped there. "I'm tired," she said. I'll try to sleep now."

Chon lowered the volume on the radio. He shook his head and rubbed his eyes to ready himself for the dark, silent drive ahead of him. Then he looked over at Araceli. Having her there next to him, comfortable enough in his presence not only to have him drive her father's car, but to turn over and sleep with him roughly a foot away, made Chon want to rise to the occasion. He wanted to live up to being handed the keys and told all these secrets. He adjusted the rear-view mirror to get a better view of the road behind him.

"And Chon," Araceli said, scaring him. "I care about you."

Chon didn't immediately remember the conversation they'd had so recently. The words Araceli said were enough to make him forget about anything she had said before she said them. She turned her head to the side, like she was talking to the ceiling of the cab.

"And Henry cares about you." Now Chon remembered. "You're cared about."

She went back to resting her head on the seat and trying to sleep.

"Thanks," Chon said. She didn't say anything back.

Realitos is a town even smaller than Greenton, the last town you pass on Texas Highway 359 before you get to Greenton. Chon drove through it after midnight, remembering that the last road in town on the way home has a small church at its end, just a block off the highway. He crossed himself with his right hand as he entered the home stretch. There was only a sliver of a moon glowing in the sky. If it were daytime, Chon would be able to see the water tower standing over the east side of town and carrying all of Greenton's barely potable water in a tank with the town's name and running Greyhound logo painted on the side. He was looking up at the sky in front of the glow of the car's headlights when he noticed the glow receding. The glow of the instrument panel and even the turquoise LCD glow of the time on the car's radio unit began dimming too. Chon tried not to panic.

Then the engine died and the steering and brakes locked up. There would certainly have been an accident if the Suburban were not the only vehicle on the road. Chon had to use all of the strength he could force into his hands to pull onto the side of the road. The sudden change in speed and Chon muttering *fuck, fuck, fuck* woke Araceli.

"What's wrong," she asked. "What's happening?"

"It turned off on me," Chon said, his heart pounding so hard he could feel its rhythm on his dry throat. "It just died."

133

"Is it the battery?" Araceli adjusted her seatback so that she was sitting upright. She looked groggy but no longer frightened.

"No," Chon said. "Well, yes. But the battery wouldn't die while the engine is on." Chon tried the key in the ignition. The starter was clicking in futility. "It's the alternator."

"Can you fix it?"

"No. I'm not even 100% sure that's what it is," Chon admitted.

Araceli leaned her head on the window beside her and closed her eyes, like she wanted five more minutes of sleep before getting up to face the day.

"Okay," she said and sat up. "I'll call my dad. My mom made me bring her cell phone in case of an emergency."

"Smart lady," Chon said. The fact that Araceli had a phone to call for help calmed him. He hadn't released the steering wheel from his sweaty grip. He let go and rubbed his hands on his jeans and tried to slow his breathing.

Araceli dialed a number. After a while, she pressed the 'end' button on the phone and put it down on her lap.

"Shit!" she said. "I think he might still be at the fence job by Zapata. It went straight to voicemail. There's no reception down there."

"So no Henry either?" Chon asked.

"What would he do if we called him anyway?" She had a point.

"So are you going to try your house? Maybe he's there and his phone is off."

"Yeah, but maybe he's not and my mom will answer and panic. She could come get us, but she doesn't know anything about cars and my father would kill both of us if we left the Suburban out here. Can we call your house?" she asked.

"My dad knows less about cars than your mom does." Chon was starting to feel nervous.

"Okay then," Araceli said and dialed a number in the phone so quickly as to indicate muscle memory in her thumb from having dialed it too many times to count. She brought the phone to her ear.

While it was ringing, Chon asked, "Who are you calling?"

Araceli was listening hopefully to the line. Her answer was short. "A mechanic."

The conversation Araceli had on the phone was short.

"Mr. Mejia," she said. "It's me."

"I'm fine. I'm fine," she reassured him. "The reason I'm calling is I'm having car problems. Yeah. Hold on." She covered the phone with her hand and asked Chon where they were. He told her. "We're just outside Realitos. About five miles. The car just turned off. We think it's the alternator. Yeah. Okay. Thank you so much. See you soon."

She put the phone down and rubbed her eyes and shook her head.

"He'll be here as soon as he can," she told Chon. He nodded, indicating that he thought this to be a good thing. "Are you okay?" she asked him. "You seemed pretty freaked out there for a while."

Chon put the headrest behind him to use. He let out a long exhalation of relief. "I really was," he told her. "I'm just glad you knew the home number to a mechanic who would come out and help us in the middle of the night."

"Yeah, well..." Araceli started but didn't finish.

"And how about you?" Chon asked into the silence of the sentence Araceli let die. "You seemed pretty freaked out yourself when you woke up. Are you okay?"

"Yeah, I'm fine. I'm just glad you were driving. I would have probably started screaming and crying and run the car off the road." Araceli laughed a little at this thought.

"You might have cried and screamed," Chon said. "But you wouldn't have run the car off the road. I had to fight the damn thing to park it here. We were a couple of seconds from being half-parked in the road."

"Oh Chon, you saved the day," Araceli joked. "My hero." She reached over and laid a soft palm on Chon's face. She was flashing a good-spirited smile to go with the playful tone she had set up.

The gesture froze Chon and scrambled his brain a little. He looked over at her, eying her hand on his face. Then he looked at her hard, letting her know he wasn't capable of joking right then because of what her touch, what she, was doing to him—what she always did to him. She took back her hand—Chon could see clearly even in the near black of the starless night around them that she looked down and blushed.

This was where a smoother guy would say something to win the moment for romance. But Chon couldn't come up with the anything at all to say, let alone the right thing. Later he was glad that the paralysis wasn't limited to just his voice, because all he could think to do at that moment was grab her—grab her and squeeze her and, for as long as she allowed it, come as close to occupying the same space with her as possible. Would she have recoiled? Would all his hopes for winning her have been left to die on the side of the road?

Yes. He had readied himself for heartbreak from the onset of his pursuit of Araceli.

In the end, his inaction seem prudent and considerate and prescient. Just minutes later, Andres Mejia passed them on the highway going in the direction of Realitos, only to slow down, make a U-turn, and park his truck behind them on Texas Highway 359 southbound.

Araceli jumped out of the car. Chon sat and watched in the side-view mirror as Andres got down from his truck—a slender man made to look big for all of his muscles—

and very delicately leaned down a little to wrap his arms around Araceli. They spoke for a bit. He said something that made her laugh, and they came up to the car. Chon opened the car door a crack when they came close.

"Pop the hood," Andres instructed him.

Chon did. He joined them in front of the car. Andres handed Chon a flashlight wordlessly and placed his toolbox on the ground. He worked the hood's latch, then opened it and set it up on its prop rod. He held a hand out to Chon, who placed the flashlight in it. He shone the light onto the car's internal organs and poked at the alternator belt. He reached into his toolbox and pulled out a couple of small wrenches. With these, he loosened one of the battery cables from its terminal. Then he grabbed a crescent wrench. He adjusted it to fit a bolt on a pulley through which the belt ran. He stuck it in and—with one hand, like he expected it to be easy—gave the wrench a turn. It didn't budge.

"Damn," he said. He tried again, pulling with both hands. "Okay, I'm going to need your help."

Chon expected to be asked to hold the flashlight, but Andres handed it to Araceli.

"The self-tensioner is sticking. I'll have to use both hands to loosen it so what I want you to do is slide that belt off the pulley when I do. Easy as that, just pull it off the track." For the first time, Andres looked at Chon. He spoke quietly and patiently. "Can you do that?"

"Sure," Chon said. He leaned in to better reach the belt.

Andres gave a nod and pulled the wrench back. When the tension loosened, Chon pulled at the belt.

"See," Andres said, not looking at Chon. "That was easy."

He got the flashlight back from Araceli and examined the belt.

"Cracked," he said. "You're in luck. I think I have one this size in the truck."

He walked back to his truck toolbox and rooted around it, finally pulling out a new belt. He examined it and compared its size and length with the old one. Meanwhile, in front of the Suburban, both Araceli and Chon watched him, neither saying a word and neither looking at one another. Convinced that it was a right fit, Andres brought the belt to the Suburban. He snaked it around the proper pulleys and gears and brought it back up to the top.

"We're doing the same thing." His eyes seemed intimidating, but not challenging. "Only this time in reverse."

He pulled back on the crescent wrench, straining to hold it there. When Chon finally got the belt over, Andres eased the tensioner into place. He pressed down on the newly installed belt.

"Good job," he said. He replaced the battery cable, then started walking back to his truck.

"That's it?" Araceli asked.

"Almost," he said. "Try the key."

Chon got in the car and turned it on. Nothing. Andres was back, holding a jump starter in his hand.

"That's what I thought," he said. "You ran your battery dead. I'll start it up and when you get home, leave it running for about twenty minutes." He connected his machine to the car.

"Now," he said.

Chon turned the car on. Andres closed the hood.

Araceli and Andres stood outside, a thin pane of glass separating them from Chon. Chon tried to pretend like he couldn't hear every word they were saying.

"Thank you so much for coming. I don't know what I would have done," Araceli said.

"It's not a problem. I'm just glad you called."

"How much does my dad owe you?"

"Mi 'ja, don't embarrass me. I can't charge you." Andres put down the jumpstarter he'd been holding. "What are you guys doing for Thanksgiving?"

"Going up to Houston to see my uncle," Araceli told him.

"Your uncle Marky?" Andres said, giving a little bit of a laugh. "I thought him and your mom were fighting."

"Yeah, they were. But they got over it."

"That's good. Tell them both I say hello. And Christmas?" he asked. "Will you guys be in town for Christmas?"

"I think so."

"It would be great if you'd come visit. She would really appreciate it. We both would." Here, Chon had to look at Andres, if even only briefly. He met Andres' expectant eyes and turned back to staring at the steering wheel, embarrassed.

"Of course, I'll go over," Araceli said in a tone like it was ridiculous for him to have even asked. "Of course."

"Good," Andres said, then turned to walk back to his truck. Araceli walked with him. They stopped behind the Suburban and talked for a bit.

In the rear-view mirror, Chon saw a man who could well be described as handsome, perfectly built—his graying hair and wrinkling skin only adding a dignified air to his look. It was in that stance—arms crossed at the chest, right knee locked and left knee bent, left toe planted on the ground behind him, its foot probably wagging like he was waiting for a pitch—but not so much in his similarly-built muscular frame, that Chon saw John. John used to stand like his father.

This is what John would have come to look like as an adult, as a grown up.

In fact, John could have ended up like this, like his father. He might not have gone on to play professional baseball. He could have easily gone on to sustain some freak injury or to flunk out of school—undrafted and unaffiliated with any team or club, only to try his luck and fail at tryouts in the minor leagues. Or, almost unimaginable and incongruent to the idea John had made of himself and all of town had made for him, he could have gone on to fall out of love with baseball. He had fallen out of love with Araceli enough to break up with her, proving that the fairy tale that was written for him in life and cemented for him in death was just that. It was a fable, a myth that represented what people in town wanted regardless of what the boy might actually have come to do—or want to do—in life.

John might have gone on to become a mechanic or a librarian or an English teacher. He could have done anything. Except that now his options had been cut short. The narrative of what he might have been, the story of him, had turned into who the boy was.

Chon felt bad for John. He would have given anything just then for John and Robe to be alive—for them to fulfill the prophesies of a whole town's expectations. Or for them to fail or to quit or to do something altogether different. Chon would even have given up the ground he'd gained with Araceli. The way it was now John Mejia and John Robison would never be left to rest in peace because they had parts to play in the fantasies of everyone in Greenton. John Mejia would never get the chance to choose whether or not to be a mechanic, whether or not to walk in the footsteps of his father, the father he looked so very much like.

Araceli got in the car and buckled her seat belt. She blew into her hands and rubbed them together like it was colder than 69˚ outside. She looked back at the headlights of Andres Mejia's truck. Finally she looked at Chon.

"He's waiting for you," she said. "He's going to follow me home to make sure there are no more problems with the car."

Chon okayed this and, using his blinker to indicate his intentions, pulled onto the highway and headed for home. Andres followed closely, driving at 75, making Chon have to speed up to not be rear-ended or overtaken.

"I'm sorry," Araceli told Chon who was looking in the rear-view more than the road in front of him.

"For what?"

"Back there, I didn't mean to have a whole conversation with him while you waited in the car."

"Oh, it's fine."

"And I'm sorry if he was kind of rude to you. I don't think he was ready to come out and find me with a guy in the middle of the night."

"Did you tell him we just went to the game?" Chon asked, wondering if some sort of explanation or excuse should have been offered. Judging by the way Andres was driving, the whole situation might not have come off as couth per the Mejia handbook of propriety and chivalry. Chon comforted himself in the knowledge that there was no way the man would run him off the road while Araceli was in the passenger seat.

"Yeah, of course, but still. Anyway, don't take it personally. He's just real protective of me. I think more because of my relationship with his wife than what John and I had."

"So, she's really that bad?" Chon asked.

"Yeah. I mean, can you blame her?"

"No, of course not. She's allowed to be sad forever, to cry 24/7 for the rest of her life if she wants to. But it seems like she's getting beat by the same thing, over and over again. She's going to wake up tomorrow and be as sad as she was yesterday. It'll be like that every day until she gets over it. And she may never." Chon looked over at Araceli, Greenton High School passing by them in the passenger window behind her.

"That's why I go. Because it's too much for one woman to take," Araceli said.

Chon nodded and turned right on Viggie, not bothering to come to a complete stop at the stoplight now blinking red.

"And if she never gets over it?" he said.

Araceli looked at Chon like she knew what he was saying but couldn't believe he'd said it, not because he was out of line, but because she didn't want to hear it.

"I guess I'll keep going over," she said.

Chon pulled the car as far into the driveway as it would go with his parents' cars in front of it. He put the car in park and looked at over at Araceli.

"Then you're letting it beat you too. Over and over again. Like her, but not really."

She got out of the car and was halfway around the front of the Suburban by the time Chon had opened the door next to him. He got out and stood before Araceli, the hi-beams of Andres' Chevy casting shadows of the two of them on Chon's house.

"Thanks for coming and getting me for the game," Chon told her.

"Thanks for riding with me." Araceli looked up at Chon with a sadness he was now allowed to see in her eyes.

Chon made to walk away, but Araceli stopped him and pulled him into a hug. It was a small gesture, the kind shared between hormonal-but-platonic teenagers in the lunchroom at school. Chon gave Araceli a tight squeeze. He let go of her before she let go of him. He looked down at her and she put her forehead on his chin.

"Thanks," she said, "for tonight, for everything."

She got in the Suburban. Its taillights let Andres know she was backing out of the driveway. She did a quick two-point turn and drove away, not once taking her eyes off of

Chon until he was standing, alone, on his front lawn, the darkness almost erasing in his mind all that had happened. He went inside, took off his clothes, and dreamed of John Mejia thirty years in the future, still alive and looking just like his father, trying to run over Chon, sweaty and panicked, as he fled away down Main Street.

The Greyhound baseball team is comprised entirely of young men who played and started for the football squad, making the transition from football to baseball season simple, like going from fall to spring semester. The switch is a seamless one, whether the kid identifies as a football or baseball player. But while the sons of Greenton are signed up for football as kids and taken to practices and cheered for and encouraged to learn rules and strategies, it is a borrowed sport—one rented, like the pads and helmet that protect and make the boys feel big, but that have to be returned at the end of the season.

Greentonites own baseball. In a town whose population sees itself as being too Mexican to connect to football and too American to do the same with soccer, baseball is the sports equivalent of Tejano music. Tejano music comes in the bastardized Spanish lexicon Greentonites find familiar and comfortable, even those whose first-learned and primarily-used language is English. Its accordions and synthesizers and sometimes country shuffle are distinctly Mexican and American, with none of the tubas or nasal norteño pitch and phrasing that mark banda or the antiquated standup bass and acoustic guitars of danzón.

So it is with baseball. There are Hernandezes and Lopezes and Valenzuelas in professional baseball who could be rooted for even if they aren't necessarily Mexican because Mexican Americans aren't necessarily Mexican either. They often see themselves as having a closer connection to Cubans or Puerto Ricans or Panamanians than with their own Caucasian countrymen who themselves might see a brown Gonzales or Mejia or Monsevais—Texas, America, born and raised—as having more in common with foreigners too.

Baseball is the easiest and most natural sport for Greentonites to latch onto. It is the brand new glove they buy, rub with shaving cream, wrap with a large rubber band around a few balls, and leave in the sun one morning to retrieve worn, loose, and ready that evening. It's used until the stitching breaks and falls apart, when they'll get a new one and give it the same love and care, never throwing out the old one, but keeping it on a shelf or in a drawer or in a box in the garage labeled 'old stuff.'

For the cream of Greenton's baseball crop, baseball season never ends. There's a summer league that starts at the end of Little League's playoffs, causing some boys to play for both their summer squads and Greenton's all-star team should the team have advanced beyond regional play. This is an exhilarating possibility. The boys who fall into such circumstances will likely go on to play together from then on, representing the town of Greenton against teams from around the area and even around the state in those all-star tournaments and then in high school, with everyone in town, not just their friends and families, watching and cheering them on. If their parents have the means, like the Robisons and the Mejias before them, if there were a boy or two who proved themselves special enough and dedicated enough and destined enough for a future of greatness—or at least a chance at it—they would be signed up for traveling autumn and winter league teams made up of the region's other elite baseball mercenaries. Their SUV and mini-van driving parents would travel from town to town to watch them play against other bands of baseball junkies and phenoms and kids whose glory-hungry parents had dollar signs in their eyes and dreams in their hearts of better lives for their kids than they'd gotten from their own parents.

There was only one such ball player on the 1999 Greenton High School baseball team. He was a switch-hitting second baseman who could pitch an inning or two of relief if needed with a less than overwhelming—but still off-putting—knuckle ball that he had to complement a decent two-seam fastball. He was a freshman, starting varsity, of course.

On the day of Greenton's first game, he stood in front of one of the mirrors in the school's locker room taking in the sight of himself in a brand new uniform, bought with John-star money. The button-up green shirt and green pinstriped white pants looked good, better than any uniform he'd ever worn. But with the '8' embroidered on the left arm of the jersey and the '34' on the left, he felt cheated. He was four years younger than the Johns. He had met them and cheered them on. Both of them had taken an interest in his progress, giving him suggestions on his stance and swing in the batter's box.

But four years? Why not three? Wearing the jersey that bore the numbers of the Johns made him stand tall. He promised himself that he would do all that he could to live up to the colors he was wearing and to the fact that he'd just inherited the team from the Johns. He would play as hard as he could to honor their memory. He was proud of the mission he'd charged himself with, but still he felt cheated by the year that separated him from having played with them. He couldn't wait to dirty his new uniform with the orange red dirt on the diamond that was being watered and raked thick and crackly, ready to crunch under foot like he wanted to believe snow would crunch if ever he actually walked on it. He put on his cap. He was a superhero donning his mask and cape, a king his crown and scepter. He was no longer a student athlete, no longer a baseball player. He *was* baseball. Walking away from the mirror, his cleats click-clacking

on the concrete floor of the locker room, the young second baseman, still a week shy
of his fifteenth birthday, felt something welling up in the deepest recesses of his being.
It was a surge of emotion at reaching this new milestone, pride at taking the field
a Greyhound, regret at not being able to do have done so with the Johns, profound
sadness at their passing. He was not mature enough to recognize what he was going
through. If he was, he would have to ignore it because you're not allowed to think of
anything but winning before a baseball game. And you're not allowed to feel pain from
anything but an injury in a locker room.

Coach Gallegos led his second baseman and a squad of fourteen other boys —who
would do nothing over the next four years to make names for themselves—to the main
entrance of the stadium and showed them the bronze plaques that had been forged
in the Johns' likenesses. He told them about life being more important than baseball
and about baseball being larger than life. He told them about winning and losing and
playing with heart. He charged his players to, "do it for the Johns."

A half-time or pre-game speech this was not. He could hear himself sounding
like a fool. The rest of his career would be defined in contrast to the four years he had
with the Johns, which themselves would stand, like the boys' images on the plaques
that now adorned the entrance to Greenton's baseball stadium, in relief of every
other squad he ever coached or played on. He would coach winning teams again. The
Greyhounds would make playoff runs. But no team, no player, no era would ever match
what the Johns had given him, given Greenton. Baseball was everything to him. The
Johns' dying couldn't take that from him. But his passion for coaching wasn't the same
anymore. His world had changed.

First pitch was scheduled for 11 am. People filed in an hour before. The stands
weren't full, but there were more people there than normally show up for a Saturday

morning pre-season exhibition game against a Santa Rosa team who wasn't very good. They would face them three more times in the regular season anyway.

But people had heard there would be an unveiling of a couple of plaques in the Johns' likenesses. They had expected the plaques to be covered, like the crucifix at church during Holy Week, but there was no such affectation.

Eight months had passed since the accident. Things had settled down. The calm of Greenton that had been disturbed was now restored. People were mostly over the tragedy. What good would another awkward tribute have done anyone outside of the families of the dead boys? The Robisons were gone, and the Mejias had no intention of showing up at the stadium that day to be walked out to home plate to wave at people clapping.

But no one in the audience knew that. After stopping to admire the plaques as they walked in, they thought that the Mejias would surely be there. They also thought the show would be more than just five innings of lopsided baseball. The game, however, ended early on account of the ten-run rule. Four of the Greyhounds' runs were batted in by the fourteen-year-old second baseman phenom. His parents were in the stands to answer the questions that started floating around. "Who is that kid? What are ya'll feeding him?"

"Domingo," the proud parents answered. "He loves baseball. He's loved it since he could walk."

It was February 13th, the day before Valentine's day. The people in the crowd were disappointed in the Mejia-sighting that had not come to pass. But this Mingo kid...he put on a show for them. Their allegiances shifted that day, as they would have with the Johns off to UT, death or not. They had not seen a train wreck, but they had found their new man. It was a good day, February 13th 1999—one for moving on.

SPRING

Chon was not at the Greyhounds' season opener against Santa Clara that Saturday. It was a long weekend—school was out Monday for a teacher workday—and the only weekend that Chon would spend without Araceli since the night of the first football game of the season.

On Christmas, she and Chon and Henry had stolen away to Henry's house with beer, pan de polvo, tamales, and a plate of mole pilfered from Araceli's home party.

The three of them rang in the New Year at a party at the Lazo ranch, just past the cemetery. It was populated with high school students from both Greenton and Falfurrias and many alumni who had caught wind of something brewing out on Fal Street. There was a palpable animosity coming from the circle of automobiles around the fire. It made Chon uncomfortable. So they left and fired Roman candles and threw bottle rockets at each other at the county line—having as much fun as any children ever let to run around and play with explosives in the dead of night. They listened to the countdown on the radio. When 1999 came in, the station played the Prince song. Araceli hugged Henry and gave Chon the slightest of pecks on his unsuspecting lips. Henry seemed more surprised by this than Chon, but he played it off by making fun of Chon's clearly elated state and his ear-to-ear grin. It was dark, and the three of them were alone in the middle of nowhere. They used the rest of their fireworks to light the darkness around them, and then they drove back home.

Whether he worked or not, whether Henry was around to serve as a now unnecessary buffer between his cousin and his best friend, Chon spent at least one night of every weekend with Araceli. Seeing how he treated her confidences, she opened up to him more, sharing her plans for the future.

She had pinned her hopes on UT. She had pictures cut out of brochures thumb-tacked to the corkboard above the desk in her room. She did her homework there, checking her answers twice in hopes of getting to that huge university with green lawns and over a century of traditions she badly wanted to be a part of. She had applied in October and was waiting for a response, hoping for the right one.

Chon thought UT would be nice. Anywhere with Araceli would be nice. But he missed the admissions deadline. That meant more time at the Pachanga this summer and fall. They watched movies together and talked music.

There was another band from Austin: Fastball. Neither of them were too wowed by the album she bought. They listened to it driving around in her father's Suburban. There was one song—their big hit—about a couple leaving for a trip and never making it back. Araceli looked over at Chon when she heard it and shook her head. She pulled the truck into the post office parking lot and started laughing so hard she grabbed at her sides and sank into her seat a little bit. He laughed too, and then she cried. He gave her a conciliatory pat on the back, and she leaned over the center console and put her head on his shoulder.

Then it happened. It happened again, really. But this time it felt more real, like it counted. She put her left hand on Chon's face and turned it to her so that she could kiss him. Like on New Year's, it was small—intimate, but close to asexual. Had the circumstances been at all different, had Araceli not just been crying over the death of her first love, Chon would have seized the opportunity and let out four years of frustrated passion.

But no such thing happened. Araceli's crying before she kissed him was unsettling enough, but the burst of pouts and tears she let out right after she kissed him made Chon feel like he had done something wrong—like all the time they'd spent together during the last several months had brought them to this place that Araceli wasn't ready for. She pulled away, getting as far from him as she could in the front seat of the Suburban. She hid her face where the window next to her met the door, crying for a while longer before throwing the car into gear and driving Chon back home. They didn't say a word the whole way, just bye when he got out.

This was on Thursday. At school on Friday, Araceli apologized to Chon for "freaking out," begged him to forgive her for it right then and to forget about it forever after. He forgave her, and that was that. He asked what she was doing that weekend, knowing it was Valentine's and a long weekend and hoping that her response would be that she would like to be with him. But she was going to Corpus with her family to visit the Velas, not to return until Monday to get ready for school the next day.

So that settled that. For once, he had free weekend time. Ana had been asking to pick up extra shifts. He was happy to give her his weekend hours now that he had something to do, someone to be with. Except that this weekend he didn't.

He woke up feeling lonely. He called Henry's, but Henry's dad picked up, sounding bothered at the thought of the phone ringing before noon. He said Henry was sleeping. Chon didn't want to sit around in his room, a room he had come to detest because it reminded him of the sad hours he'd spent there when he had nowhere else to go. He got dressed, fired up the Dodge-nasty, and headed west by northwest for Laredo.

He drove the fifty-six miles of Texas Highway 359 that separated Greenton from the nearest city—not exactly sure what he was doing or where he was going. Warm, dry air blew through his hair and stung his eyes. Then he had an idea, one so perfect he wasn't sure if he had known it the whole time or not. How could he have gotten in the car and headed for Laredo without intending to buy Araceli a Valentine's gift?

He headed for Mall del Norte. He rifled through the contents of the glove compartment and found a checkbook he'd gotten from the credit union but never used. He tore a few checks out (numbers 1, 2, and 3), folded them in half, and slipped them into his wallet. He was going to buy Araceli a proper Valentine's gift. It might be something she would love or like or maybe not even want. But with it, Chon was going to abandon all pretenses and make his intentions—however obvious they may have already been—clear, out there for her to take or leave.

No matter what the gift, he would put his friendship with Araceli—and maybe even his friendship with Henry—on the line. It was a risk, a scary one. But Chon believed that he wasn't acting selfishly. After all, she needed to know exactly how he felt. He knew she was asking herself questions about the two of them, questions that needed answering. He saw it in Araceli's eyes when they met each morning at school and when they parted after a night of killing time.

What he was doing was right.

He sat there sweating in the car. He closed his eyes and saw Araceli.

What he was doing was right.

Chon opened the Pachanga on Monday. As had been his practice all year long, Rocha took Chon's day off from school to mean that Chon would be available to open the store and Rocha would be able to drink cheap beer and fortified wine in the dirt alley behind his house with the old drunks he knew as kids who would always come around when they heard a beer can crack open or a tin cap scraping glass signifying that wine was about to flow. They sat in lawn chairs and on milk crates, blocking the cars that weren't ever going to pass by.

Chon didn't mind opening up. In fact, it was perfect for him—he wouldn't have to work until near midnight, which would be too late to go over to Araceli's on a school night. He would get off of at three, shower and change. Then he could take Araceli his gift.

The Pachanga was busier than normal. Tryouts and team drafts were being held at the Little League field. Chon's parents were there with Pito, who was excited in a way that seemed strange to Chon. He was fired up about baseball—the game, the sport—not about going out and playing grabass with his friends and picking flowers in left field. He wasn't a tee-baller anymore. When did the kid get old enough to be passionate about something?

There was a steady stream of kids coming into the store and buying Gatorades (the boys in their gray polyester pants and baseball caps) and sodas (their little brothers and sisters). When Ana came to work at two-thirty, the cooler shelves had holes. Chon gave the floors a quick sweep-up, then grabbed his jacket and headed into the cooler.

After a while, the bell above the cooler door rang. Ana needed help in front. Chon looked out at the store between the drinks. There didn't seem to be too many people for Ana to handle. Maybe she had gotten a phone call she needed to take. He stuck his head, red-faced and burning earlobes, out of the cooler door and looked at Ana inquisitively.

"I think you've got a visitor, Chones." Ana nodded in the direction of the Suburban parked in front of the store.

There she was, hair pulled back and sunglasses sitting on top of her head. She was putting on lipstick in the visor-back mirror in front of her. Watching her like that, without her knowing, without her having to act interested or keep at a safe distance, Chon felt good. Ana rang up the only customer she had, an old man buying some chicarrones and a topo chico. He had looked over at Araceli in the parking lot when Chon came out.

"You're a lucky guy," he said in Spanish. "She's putting on makeup." Then he said something else, fast and singsong, like an old saying or joke. He left, laughing to himself.

Chon thought about asking Ana what the guy had said, but he wasn't sure if he wanted it repeated, least of all by her. Chon looked at the clock: five more minutes.

"Just go," Ana told him. "I'll punch you out." She was smiling, proud almost. He didn't know what that smile meant, only that it didn't look cruel. It looked generous, caring, like she was giving Chon the only thing she had worth offering.

"He's right," she said as he took off his jacket and hung it on the hook next to the cooler door. "She's putting on that makeup for you. Who else does she have to look good for here?"

"That's what he said?"

"Yeah, that and some other stuff." She laughed and walked out from behind the register to empty the coffee pots and brew fresh ones.

Chon signaled to Araceli to wait a second when he came out. He ran to the Dodge-nasty. When he came back, he climbed onto the passenger seat of the Suburban, closed the door, and put on his seat belt.

"Hey," Araceli said.

"Hey. You want to go for a ride?" he asked, the box in his pocket too small to be seen in the bagginess of his pants but making him feel exposed nonetheless.

She threw the truck into gear. "I was about to ask you the same thing."

"How was Corpus?" Chon asked.

"Good. Really good. I'm glad I went. They're really good people, the Velas. I got to do a little shopping and even went with my family to a show at the place I told you about."

"The place with the surfboards?"

"Yes! We just went, we didn't even know who was playing. And, guess what?" She paused here, actually wanting him to guess.

"It was closed?"

"No, stupid. Bob Schneider was playing. Can you believe that? He was down from Austin, playing to promote a new album. It was amazing."

"So you took you parents to show them this place where this thing happened this summer" —Araceli had pulled out of the Pachanga heading for the 'Y.' She took the turnaround and had already driven across town. She pulled onto the shoulder of the highway to let cars pass by so she could make a U-turn and drive across town again— "and the same guy is playing when you get back? That's pretty crazy."

"I know," Araceli said. "When I saw the marquee, I gave this scream-shout thing. I couldn't believe it. We had dinner there and stayed for the show. I was so happy."

"Araceli, that's perfect."

"After the show," she said. "We stuck around, and I bought his new album. It's really good."

"Put it on," Chon said.

They rode for a while just listening to the music. She turned around at the 'Y' again, but when she reached the north end of town, she just kept going. Chon wanted her to keep going, to let Highway 16 turn to Freer and then to San Antonio and then to forever.

"Isn't it good?" she asked. "Isn't it just perfect?"

"Yes," Chon said. But he was lost, trying to feel every bit of right then.

Araceli looked over at him.

"Yes," he said again. "This is perfect."

"Perfect," she repeated. They rode on.

Araceli turned the music down a bit.

"Open the glove box there."

Chon did and found a CD still wrapped in cellophane.

"I thought you might like it, so I bought you a copy. So, you know, happy Valentine's Day."

Chon looked at the CD in his hands. The album cover was a black and white cubist portrait. On the back was a track listing and a picture of the band.

Chon looked over at Araceli, beautiful behind her sunglasses. "I got you something too," he told her.

She lifted her sunglasses over her forehead. "Shut up," she said.

"Really, I did," Chon said, reaching in his pocket for the box.

Araceli pulled the Suburban onto the side of the road, a smile on her face.

He produced the box, a small one—obviously holding jewelry. She stopped smiling. Chon tried not to notice. He held it out to her, but she didn't take it.

"What is it?" she asked.

"Open it," he told her, but he quickly realized she wasn't going to.

He opened it for her, revealing a teardrop-shaped blue marble glass pendant. She looked at it and at Chon. She didn't seem angry or even upset. Just blank. She looked out of the window next to her and then put her head on the steering wheel. Chon closed the box and laid it on the dashboard between his side of the cab and hers.

"Happy Valentine's Day," he said, like he had meant to but feeling stupid for it.

He sank down in his chair and looked away from Araceli. She put the car in gear and turned around to head home.

"Why?" she asked. Before he could answer—as he had prepared to do in case she ask that very question—she continued. "Why does it always have to be something? Why does it have to go somewhere? I like you, Chon," she said. She waited for him to turn. "I like you a lot. But isn't it just easier to not make it something?"

"So you want me to just pretend—" Chon said loudly, sitting up like he was getting ready for a battle.

"Yes." She cut him off. "I want you to just pretend. I want you to pretend like you don't feel what you feel and I don't feel what I feel. I want you to pretend I never kissed you, like you don't look at me the way you do. If I can pretend, then why can't you?"

"Because it's bullshit. Why should I lie to myself? Why should we lie? Because it's easier? That's bullshit. I have wanted to be with you for a really long time. And I knew I was probably never going to have a chance with you under normal circumstances, but I got the chance. I got to spend time with you, and I learned how much I really do like you—you, not what you look like or how popular you are. And, even crazier than anything else, you like me. So why not try? Why not get you a cheap piece of jewelry and give it to you, praying that you want it, that you'll want what it means?"

"Oh, I don't know," Araceli said, her voice breaking. "Because it would just totally fuck up my whole world for the next three months, maybe? Everybody will talk."

"They already talk," Chon said.

"You don't understand what it's like," she said.

"We've been hanging out all year," he told her. "You don't understand. You're so used to everyone staring at you and paying attention to you that you don't notice it anymore. I'm used to being invisible, but I've gotten used to being seen. It wasn't easy and I don't like it, but I got used to it."

They caught a red at the stoplight as they pulled into town. There was a car next to them, full of kids who were classmates of Chon and Araceli. Every single head in the car was turned toward them. Araceli Monsevais was crying and that guy she'd been hanging out with lately seemed to have made it happen. They stared, their mouths dropped open

"Well, then, you don't know what it'll be like for me," she said. "You can't say you know what it'll be like for me."

The light turned green. Araceli peeled out, leaving the kids to cross through the intersection at a lazy, day-off-from-school pace, talking about what they'd seen, guessing what it could have meant, making up a handful of stories and arguing about which one was most likely to be true as they drove up and down Main until dinner time. Araceli pulled into the Pachanga parking lot. She parked the Suburban behind the store, catty-corner to the drive up window.

"I guess I just figured that however hard it would be on you, it would be easier because we would be together," Chon told her.

He got out of the Suburban. In an attempt to not slam the passenger door in anger, he hadn't closed it properly. He opened it and shut it again. It was hot out. It reminded him that he was corporeal, not just a walking ball of feelings. His body, now with him again, felt weak. He wanted to drive home where he could get into bed to rest his hurting bones. He had left the necklace on the dashboard.

Araceli opened her door and stepped out.

"Your CD," she said. "You forgot your CD."

She climbed down from her seat and met him where he stood. She held out the gift. When he grabbed it from her with both hands, she kissed him. He looked down at her, searching her eyes for some indication of what it meant. Was she going to cry again? Was this the kind of kiss that signals the end of something that never was. Or was it the other, better, harder to define kind?

In her eyes, he found his answer. He wrapped his arms around her, and she held onto him—looking up at him, trying to register all of the information that was being relayed and process all of the changes that would result from the look that they were sharing. It meant not only that they were together. It meant she was not alone. It was her fear—when she had considered being with Chon—that he would confuse the two, that he might feel that she was with him just to be with someone so she wasn't alone. But he showed her then that he knew the difference, he understood she wanted to be with him and that made whatever they would come to face in town small and manageable, almost even negligible. Almost.

"Wait," she said.

She went to the Suburban, turned up the music, and grabbed his gift.

"Help me put this on," she said. She handed him the box. He took the necklace out and unclasped it. She held up her hair and he fastened the thin gold chain behind her neck.

"It's beautiful," she told him and took hold of him again.

He held her close and they danced, eyes closed, to Bob Schneider singing about the world exploding into love all around him. When the song ended, they kissed again, and then opened their eyes. There they were, back on Earth. In Greenton, in the Pachanga's makeshift employee parking lot. Of all the places to end up after coming back from a dream, they were there. But it felt better. It felt bearable. They would make it past the next three months and into whatever future lay beyond it.

Some of the houses in the southwest corner of Greenton were among the town's oldest structures, holdovers from earlier days. Their proximity to the railroad tracks was no coincidence. The town was built around those tracks, a station town where people from all over the southwest looking for a better life or for work cowboying or prospecting or roughnecking could get off to stretch their legs and maybe buy a pint of mash and maybe even look at the cactus and mesquite and scrub brush around them and then, for some reason unknown to their ancestors, decide to set up camp and make a go of the American dream.

As word got around about Greenton, about what it did and didn't have to offer, about how hard what little work there was would be, and about the rest of Southwest Texas, less and less people got off of the trains to stay. Less lines stopped over and Greenton had to move on to a new mode of economy. Shops and a town would no longer be sustained by rail station money. So the focus shifted to catering to the ranchers and oil men working the ranches and wells all around town. Feed shops and a general market popped up over on what is now Main Street. Those first shops and houses near the tracks, less than half a century after being created, began their course of running down.

As the bigger stores on Main drew people, a courthouse was built, then a school and a church. Greenton became the town that ranch folk, along with the people they hired to tend to their land and their stock, went to for schooling and doctoring and worshiping. They bought feed and supplies there.

But more than utilitarian needs were met by a town-proper popping up from what had once been just a train station and desert brush before that. Greenton's southwest side served the ranch people with an escape. It was a place to go that wasn't fenced-in by wooden posts and, later, by barbed wire. It was a place for blowing off steam. Houses turned into beer joints and brothels, meant to serve thirsty and horny workers who hadn't seen hide nor hair of anything besides cattle and pigs and goats and other men they had come to hate passionately and irrationally just for co-existing in the same part of the world, for stinking up their bunkhouses, and for not being the people they had planned on spending their lives with.

Prohibition brought townspeople—who had previously stayed away from these dens of sin—for a drink and a dance and a cheap, discrete fuck. Then repeal made the district (a few streets, really) obsolete. Piety and hypocrisy's foggy hindsight made the Greentonites look at those streets in scorn and contempt. The highways Roosevelt paid the men in the area to build that would connect the country and fix the economy were the southwest side's death knell—highways that led to San Antonio and Laredo, to drive-in theaters and to affordable Ford cars, to Chevy pickups, and to rock'n'roll. Viggie Street headed out of town to Laredo on Highway 359. It was paved and striped and, by the end of the construction, cut Greenton in half. North of it were the schools and newer homes and, later, the car dealership and grocery store. South of it at Main was 'downtown,' and the 'Y.' But just west of there, where town had started at the railroad tracks, south of 359, was the bad side of a poor town. It was one- and two-room clapboard shotgun houses, a few of which still did not have indoor plumbing. It looked like the death of something, but there was nothing to be mourned. It was just another victim of progress toward what Greenton became, which was not much. And so it was not anything worth missing.

On the Saturday after Valentine's Day, Chon woke up early and drove out to the last street in town. It was just up Viggie, the street where Chon lived, to Sigrid. He took a left on Sigrid, went over a set of railroad tracks to an unpaved red dirt road that led to the southwest side of town.

He drove slowly, barely putting his foot on the accelerator. Passing by the houses and trailer homes—parked, wheels flattened, on cement slabs in the middle of tiny, cheap, barren plots of land—Chon felt like he was in a different world. It was his world, or part of his world at least, but he did not see himself in the cracked paint and sagging frames of the houses in a neighborhood that sat, literally, around the block from his house.

He continued on the dirt road until it ended. When he got to the lot he was looking for, he was glad to see a certain Chevy conspicuously missing from its driveway. He pulled up to a garage, new and modern-looking compared to the buildings around it.

The roll-up doors were open, so he walked in. An old Pontiac rested, comatose if not cold dead, on the slick concrete floor of the garage. It was waiting to be cured, to be fixed and resurrected and given its wings back. There were big Craftsman chests full of tools that would be used in the Pontiac's operation. Chon looked up at the hoses that fed air from a compressor at the back of the workshop to the tools that now do the jobs that only muscle and sweat used to do. On the walls of the shop, there were posters advertising parts and tools, all shiny chrome, and some with short-shorted, car brand tank-topped women on them.

There was a small room in the corner of the shop. The thin wood door with the cheap plastic plate that read OFFICE on it was closed. Chon knocked. From the other side of the door, he heard loud, almost unhealthy-sounding snoring. It continued, uninterrupted by his knock. Chon knocked again, harder. The chainsaw buzz breathing continued. Chon considered leaving and coming back later, but then he ran the risk of Andres Mejia being in. He could only imagine what Andres would do if Chon came and asked him to risk his certification, his business, and a steep fine by breaking the law.

He gave the door a hard, open-palmed slam. There was a gasping sound—someone waking up and the shuffling of papers and the squeaks of an old desk chair. Goyo Mejia pulled the door open so fast that Post-it notes that had been stuck onto the wall behind him blew off.

"What the fuck, man?" he shouted. "Jesus Christ. You trying to give me a goddamn heart attack? What time is it?"

"Eight-thirty," Chon said calmly, too quietly to be heard over Goyo's panting.

"What? What fucking time is it?"

"Eight-thirty," Chon said louder.

"Eight-thirty? What the fuck are you doing in my shop at eight-thirty?" Goyo had stopped moving around frantically. He put his palm over his eyes. He rubbed them slowly and tenderly.

"Sign says you guys open at eight," Chon said.

"I know what the sign says," Goyo said, getting up from his chair. "But it's Saturday."

He walked out of the office and poured himself a cup of coffee from a pot that smelled fresh enough to Chon. Goyo nodded at the stack of Styrofoam cups next to the coffee maker. Chon shook his head no.

"C'mon, man. It's for the customers."

Chon grabbed a cup and emptied two packets of sugar and a creamer into it before pouring the coffee in. He made a swirl of varied shades of brown with the stir-straw. He took a tongue-burning sip of it for want of something to do while Goyo stood staring into the space that separated the two of them.

"Eight-fucking-thirty," Goyo said, not exactly under his breath, but with no trace of hostility directed at Chon, shaking his head as he walked out of the garage and toward Chon's car.

"So what seems to be the problem?" he asked Chon over his shoulder.

Chon was coming slowly out of the garage, holding the coffee with one hand and shielding his eyes from the morning sun with the other. He didn't hear the question. "I'm sorry, what was that?" he said. He blinked his eyes and moved his hand from his eyes. In spots and rays and sparkles, Goyo was revealed.

"I asked you—" Goyo said. His tone dropped off there. Goyo looked Chon up and down, as if working up an estimate in his head, "—what's the problem?"

Chon felt transparent. There was a look of knowing in Goyo's eyes, and Chon was forced to wonder if Goyo remembered that Chon had seen him drunk, sobbing, and bleeding on Main Street.

"With the car? What brings you to the shop today?"

"Oh, nothing. I just need to get it inspected," Chon said.

"I know that. I saw the ticket on the windshield. But what's so wrong with it that you bring it here to me, on Saturday, at eight-thirty in the morning before anyone gets here?" Goyo leaned back on the hood of the car and crossed his arms.

"Nothing, really. The parking brake doesn't work and the passenger seat belt doesn't reel in," Chon said.

Goyo's left eyebrow raised. He looked at Chon as if he was trying to divine if Chon was lying.

"Just the parking brake and the seat belt?" he asked.

"That's it," Chon told him.

"Keys."

Chon handed them over.

"Brake and seatbelt. Remember that you told me that."

"The parking brake," Chon corrected him.

Goyo looked at Chon across the roof of the car.

"Now, do you think I'd be getting in your damn car if the pedal brake didn't work?" He got in the car and drove away shaking his head.

Chon emptied his coffee in the grass. Steam rose from the ground. After a bit of time that seemed shorter than Chon would have expected it to be, Goyo drove past the garage and backed the Dodge-nasty in so quickly that Chon thought for sure he was going to hit one of the tool boxes or workbenches. It stopped with a rubber-peeling squeal of tires.

"Brakes work," Goyo said getting out of the car. He clicked on the hazard lights and walked behind the car where Chon was standing. "Lights work too. So it's just the parking brake and the seatbelt."

Chon nodded as Goyo turned off the lights and killed the engine. He walked back around the car to Chon. Tossing him the keys, he said, "She's not going to be riding shotgun, is she?"

Chon didn't understand the question. Goyo looked him hard in the eye. He pulled up a chrome stool with the Ford logo printed on its vinyl seat cover. He sat, feet propped on the bar around the stool's legs, his fingers drumming the seat underneath his crotch.

"Araceli, genius. Is Araceli going to be driving around in that death trap?"

Now Chon understood. He understood the question Goyo had asked him and he understood the way Goyo had looked at him outside, before.

"No, no. She...we..." Chon stopped and took a breath. "No. I just take it to work and school. I mean, I drop my brother off at school, that's about it."

"I don't know your brother," Goyo said. "I could give a shit if you drive him anywhere."

"Araceli and I are never in this car. She always has her dad's truck whenever we go anywhere. This thing doesn't have air or heat."

"If I give you a sticker, I better not see you driving Araceli in this heap of shit. I mean it," Goyo said, still sitting feet on stool, but no longer drumming on the seat.

"We never take this car. Ever. I promise." Chon spoke these words clearly and confidently, like he hadn't spoken any of his other words all morning.

"Good." Goyo stood up. "If I see her in your car, I'll kick your ass." He was standing right in front of Chon. Two feet separated them, but otherwise they were eye-to-eye, nose-to-nose. "I mean it. I just may fucking kill you."

Chon nodded his head. "I promise she won't ride in this car."

Goyo stood in front of Chon, staring anger at having already lost a brother and now also at the thought of losing a sister. If it didn't mean breaking his stare at Goyo—which would have meant losing a game that predates language—Chon would have looked at Goyo's hands to make sure he wasn't clutching a wrench or some other such bludgeon.

Goyo turned away and walked toward the office. "I'll get the sticker ready," he said. "That'll be $100."

It had cost Chon $80 the year before, but no one else would give him an inspection sticker on the sly—the repairs his car needed would cost four to five times that. He went to the Dodge-nasty and got his checkbook from the glove compartment.

★

Araceli got her acceptance letter to UT in late March.

In the six weeks of his relationship with her, Chon had received more attention—99% of it negative—than he ever had before in his life. It consisted mostly of dirty looks from girls and cruel befuddlement from boys. He knew that Araceli was having a rougher go of it. He was a nothing, a nobody, a dark horse no one knew was even in the race. She had an image to protect—her own and that of her dead boyfriend. Through it all, she answered the questions of *Why him?* with silence for those she didn't know well enough to give the *fuck you* she gave to everyone else. She did not once— though at times she really wanted to, she told Chon—mention that John, alive, had done her wrong. *He* had cheated on *her*. *He* had left *her*. Why tar his memory—the one held by his parents and friends, the one she herself wanted to keep, even the ideal held by the finger pointers and stone throwers who were so bent on denying her happiness? What good would it have done?

It occurred to Chon—who never told Araceli his revelation—that what she was running from when she left town the preceding summer was, in part, him. Or at least whoever would have come to fill the role of the thief of Greenton's crown jewel. She had stayed away to avoid complications like Chon, to avoid life in Greenton, which they were both learning wasn't real life. It was a world unto itself. No one outside the bounds of Greenton's 5.9 square miles or 4,498 citizens was scandalized by Araceli Monsevais having moved on from her loss. Greenton was a prescribed reality, and it was one that could be outrun.

So when Araceli received her letter of acceptance from UT with a scholarship package that meant she could get an education from the school for almost nothing, she drove straight to the Pachanga to tell Chon the good news. She handed Chon the letter and jumped up and down in excitement across the counter from him. It was a Wednesday.

All Chon really read was the letterhead: the seal of the college on top with the words written on the header, underlined in burnt orange, "The University of Texas at Austin." He caught sight of the word *Congratulations*, but he had not yet processed the word when Araceli hoisted herself over the counter and into Chon's arms. He pulled her over, her feet knocking down the barcode scanner that sat next to the register.

Her nervous energy was infectious. Three customers came in while she was there. "I just got into UT," she told them. They all left smiling, giving her their congratulations.

In his short time with Araceli, Chon had not seen that look of pure joy. It didn't infect him with happiness the way it had the customers who had come and gone.

Chon was barely smiling. The muscles in his face that pulled up the corners of his mouth hurt. It was a smile that hid and denied, like so many he had flashed when John was around. That smile hid a longing—lustful and passionate and somewhat embarrassing. This smile hid fear. He was afraid of being left behind in Greenton to spend his nights with Henry, drinking by the cemetery on the nights when he didn't have to open the store the next morning. He was afraid of losing what he had worked so hard to get, afraid of losing her.

So he smiled grimly and nodded at words he wasn't hearing as Araceli continued her celebratory jumping up and down. She danced on air there in front of him to music he couldn't hear. He felt further away from her than he ever had when he was outside of her life looking in.

The bell above the door rang. Chon turned to see who it was, painful smile still plastered on his face. It was Ana. She raised an eyebrow playfully at Chon. Araceli caught sight of her.

"Ana!" she said. "I got into UT!"

Ana looked at Araceli, who hadn't ever in her life addressed Ana directly by name—just come into the store or seen Ana around town and given the obligatory nod in lieu of a wave—then she looked at Chon. She caught wise. She looked above the stupid grin on Chon's face at the beads of sweat forming on his forehead.

"That's great mi 'jita, really wonderful."

Being there in the Pachanga with a woman he could only describe as a former lover—though he would never use those words—and the girl of his dreams made Chon feel like he did that night so long ago when, pants around his ankles and Ana on her knees in front of him, he was naked for all of Greenton to see his skinny legs and hairy, chicken cutlet ass. He felt a swell of nausea overtake him. This was all too much.

"There was a trail ride today," Ana said. "The lot was full of doolies pulling horse trailers. I swear, about fifty kids and their asshole parents, all dressed in stupid Garth Brooks shirts and cowboy hats came in here and wiped out the cooler. I didn't have a chance to get to it, so I thought I'd come and help you out."

Chon nodded. It was all he could do.

"Well, okay," Araceli said. "My mom and dad are both rushing home from work so we can celebrate. They're probably there waiting for me. I just had to come tell you the great news." She gave Chon a tender kiss on the lips. A long one with a squeeze of Chon's skinny waist, followed by a short one and her hands behind his neck, like she always gave when they parted. Ana walked into the cooler without putting on her jacket.

"I love you," Araceli said as she left.

She kept her eyes on Chon through the glass door that closed behind her.

"Love you too," he said. The words were toneless and his voice cracked a little under the weight of the phrase, but she couldn't hear that. She could only read his lips through the glass. She blew a kiss at Chon from behind the wheel of her car.

As soon as the Suburban was on its way down Main, Ana emerged from the cooler. She walked up to the counter slowly and stood looking at Chon. He was exhausted, awash in thoughts of Friday nights crashing ranch parties with Henry, getting drunk and being laughed at by kids who would not be able to imagine themselves that sad and pathetic. He didn't think he could deal with Ana just then. He knew he didn't want to.

"What?" he said harshly and without looking at Ana, almost making the word two syllables. When he did look at her, he could see she was checking herself, suppressing a reaction she normally wouldn't have thought twice about firing off. She took a deep breath.

"You got your chula," she told him. "I'm proud of you."

"This isn't funny, Ana. I'm not laughing, and so you're really just being mean right now."

"Chones, I'm not trying to be funny. Or mean. I'm just trying to talk to you. We don't talk anymore."

Chon had no response to this. He had wanted a fight just then. He wanted Ana to make jokes and mean comments so he could make some of his own—or even just yell at her. He had no response for her sincere concern. He turned around and busied himself with stocking cigarettes.

"She's a beautiful girl, and you really do deserve her. You're a good man. You're becoming a good man." Ana paused here for a response from Chon. When he gave none, she spoke on.

"She's all you've ever wanted, and you got her. Do you know how often that happens? About fucking never. People have to settle for what takes them, for whoever's settling for them. But you got your girl."

Not seeing where any of this was going, Chon finally looked Ana in the eyes. She just stood there.

"So?" he asked.

"So what are you going to do?" Ana said, herself sounding harsh now, as though she was offended by Chon's not being able to read between the very clear lines she was drawing.

"About what?"

Ana stared at Chon through the stupidity of his question.

"Well, what can I do—ask her not to go?" Chon finally said. "Ask her to put her dreams on the shelf so she can stay here in Greenton, so she can drop me off and pick me up from work and bring me lunch when she has the free time?"

"I can't tell if you're a coward or just a fucking idiot," Ana said calmly. "But I'll tell you this, you're full of shit."

There it was, the provocation Chon was looking for.

"I'm full of shit? Why, because I don't live my life for someone else, anyone else who will love me and fuck me and pay attention to me?"

Ana flashed a wide smile at this and nodded her head up and down.

"Alright," she said, still calm. "You think you have me figured out. That's cute. It really is. But you know what? I have you figured out too. See, I'm all alone. It's just me and a paycheck that barely pays the bills. I didn't finish high school, and I've only worked in shit places like this. I can't leave this town, this job. I wouldn't be able to buy enough gas to get me to any place better. And if I did go someplace better, what would I do when I got there?

"But you, you fucking pussy, you can do anything you want to. Hell, you're about to finish high school with decent grades, and you've got a girl who loves you. But you look at this situation and see no fix. You know why? Because fixing this would mean you'd have to do something big. You'd have to quit here and leave the only place you know so you can chase a girl you don't even know will stay with you. Yeah, I know you, Chones. You can't see the thing to do because you're so damn scared of being hurt and of not having home and this stupid fucking town to fall back on. I've never left here because I'm broken. You won't leave because you're afraid."

Chon said nothing to this. He stood there, steam building inside of him, trying to think of something absolutely horrible and cruel to say to Ana.

"Honestly," she said. "Why do you think you were here at the store or over at my house, fucking me when you wanted your little homecoming queen? You were too fucking scared to go after her because you didn't know what would happen. You saw me, sad and old and lonely and you hopped on. How pathetic does that make you?

"It took two boys dying for you to go after this girl. If they didn't die—" Her voice cracked here. She shook off tears that were trying to form in her eyes. She shouted, "If they didn't die, you'd still be at my house, fucking me and leaving with that sad little look on your face, like you wanted to be with anyone in the world but me."

"Yeah," Chon was finally able to shout back. "And you'd still let me fuck you."

Ana picked up a plastic chewing gum display and threw it at Chon. It caught him on the chin. Blood rolled down his neck onto his shirt. There was chewing gum all over the floor behind the counter. Ana was crying now.

"Yeah, I would. But who does that really make look sad—me or you?" She walked away from the counter, but stopped at the door.

"I really mean it," she said. "You deserve a beautiful girl like that." She spoke her last words between sobs. "Because you're a really great person. You're just such a fucking pussy. But I guess no one's perfect."

Chon stood there for a minute, staring at where Ana had been at the counter in front of him, thinking of more horrible things to say to her, trying not to hear what she had told him. He looked out at the parking lot. She was gone. He went to the restroom and washed the dried blood off his chin. He grabbed a Band-Aid from the first aid kit in the back and put it on the dent the plastic had made on his face. He picked up the gum from the floor and was able to restock the near-empty cooler between customers.

It was a slow night at the Pachanga.

The last day of school snuck up on Chon like it had on the rest of the class of '99. There were tests and projects and make-up absences to think about, but between school and work and Araceli, Chon felt like he'd lost all sense of time. He found himself wishing that the last day of school would never come. It was ironic that, after wanting school to be over for so long, Chon only thought of the next day's passing with dread. In a place where time seemed to stand absolutely still, Chon felt like all of the boring events of Greenton and high school were happening too fast. Because, come fall, Araceli would be gone.

They had talked about the fall. She was going to Austin for school. She would visit home as often as she could. When Chon could get time off from work, he would visit her. He would spend the semester working and applying for spring enrollment at UT— which he didn't believe he would get, but he didn't tell that to Araceli.

They had also made love by this point. Chon's parents were at Pito's baseball game one Saturday afternoon. Araceli came over. Chon didn't realize what was happening until it was done. Araceli told him it was better than her first time with John. With her there lying naked in his arms, Chon decided that he had had a happy childhood. None of it seemed as bad as he had made it out to be.

At work, Ana had taken to leaving early, abandoning the store completely, not bothering to lock up because she would always leave just minutes before Chon arrived. There were a couple of occasions where Chon walked into the store and there were customers walking the aisles, trying to decide what brand of unhealthy and overpriced they were going to buy that day. They never seemed to notice the store was unmanned, maybe assuming that whoever was working there was in the back or in the restroom or anywhere but a cheap clapboard house on the bad side of town. Chon couldn't tell if he actually missed Ana or if he was just feeling bad for what he told her or, even worse, if he was mad at her because she said the things she did.

That day Chon walked Araceli to her last class, the last class of high school. They parted with kisses, incredulous on-lookers be damned. He showed up to work three minutes late, almost hoping there would be a line of customers or that he would walk in on a shoplifter. Instead, he was greeted by a booze- and vomit-scratched baritone voice.

"You're late, pendejo." Rocha walked from behind the register, almost racing Chon to the time clock.

"Did Ana open today?" Chon asked. He was happy that high school was over, despite the fact that it meant Araceli was leaving him. He could manage a little bit of small talk with the old bastard.

"No," Rocha grunted. "Pinche puta quit. I've been here for ten fucking hours."

Chon was frozen there in the middle of the store by Rocha's words. He did not have time for guilt or sadness, the wind was taken out of him so wholly. Rocha walked out of the back room with his jacket draped over the forearm with the little hand on it. He looked like a waiter who was planning on spitting in your food.

"Quit?"

"She won the fucking lottery. You believe that? Hit big on one of the $20 scratch-offs. I play that shit every day, the lucky bitch." Rocha walked away shaking his head. "You need to come in to relieve me tomorrow. It's just me and you now."

"Rocha, I have graduation tomorrow. I requested the day off months ago. I'm not coming in."

"N'hombre, guey. I'm not going to work here all fucking day tomorrow. You have to come in," Rocha said, sounding satisfied at the knowledge that Chon would buckle under the weight of the situation. He opened the door to leave.

"Fuck that. I'm not coming in. If you have to work all day, if you have to close up at one, I don't care. I'm not coming in," Chon said. By the time he was done, he had raised an angry finger and was pointing it at Rocha.

"We'll see about that you little motherfucker. I'll—"

"Call Sammy if you want to. Shit, call Artie in San Antonio if you have to. I'm not coming in. Use the phone here if you don't want to pay the long distance. I'm not coming in." Chon dropped his hand and turned to walk to the back and clock in.

"You know what, you little—" Rocha started.

"Fuck you," Chon said, cutting him off again. "Go home and drink yourself blind so you can get through tomorrow, because you might have to work open to close."

Rocha tried to slam the door behind him, but the hydraulic door closer didn't let him. It shut slowly and unsatisfyingly. Chon had to laugh. He was still laughing when he got to the time card tower. It was just Rocha in the penthouse and him a few stories down. But it wasn't the sad presence of only two time cards that brought Chon down from his little high. It was the sight of an envelope behind his card. A note from Ana, he was certain.

He grabbed it with his right hand and his time card with his left. He clocked in and took the envelope behind the counter so he could open his register and get ready for what would likely be a crazy busy night.

Once he put his opening totals into the computer, Chon took the envelope out and opened it. It read:

Chones,
No hard feelings, huh? I'm glad I knew you. You really are great, remember that. I would repeat what I had said before. But I'm sure you haven't forgotten.
Let's keep the ticket thing between you and me. Don't make me pay you off.
You will never win if you don't play the game.
Ana

Chon got out to the Lazo ranch at 12:15. He was tired. He drove around outside the circle of cars, looking for Araceli's Suburban. He couldn't find it, so he parked outside the circle, near the front fence of the ranch. He could hear the voices of the kids sitting on their tailgates or dancing around the fire. He could see the flame lighting up the dark sky and painting it shades of crimson and purple.

Walking between cars, entering a world of inebriation that was kicked off hours before he got there, Chon noticed the looks from the crowd. He hadn't bothered going home to change clothes. It was too late. He was too tired. He knew that wasn't the reason for the stares, but he didn't care either way. At the New Years' Eve party, he let it all get to him. But he was happy now. He had what he wanted. If he owed an apology to anyone for getting it, it wasn't anyone there at the Lazo ranch that night. He heard Henry before he saw him.

"What a crock of bullshit!" His best friend's words were shouted, but not angrily.

Chon walked over in the direction of Henry's voice. Araceli saw him and ran to meet him with a kiss. She almost jumped on him, nearly toppling them over. She was drunk. They went over to where Henry was standing.

"And this motherfucker over here"—he gave Chon a hard slap on the shoulder, the kind he'd been giving him since they were young—"is my friend for I don't know how many years, and then he goes and fucks my cousin."

"Henry," Araceli said firmly.

"Yeah, yeah, yeah...okay. Fine. He starts dating my cousin. I mean, what the fuck?"

The people around the Suburban are laughing. It's a small, strange assembly of kids, one that showed how fickle the high school caste system had been—it had toppled just hours after the final bell. There were football players and cheerleaders and your run-of-the-mill drinkers, stoners, and nobodies, all there basking in being able to drink and laugh with the prom queen. Henry was holding court over the lot of them. It made Chon think it was a shame the two of them hadn't been more popular. It also made him realize it wouldn't have mattered. From that day on, they would know their contemporaries not by the labels they wore in high school, but as people who had been there with them, survived with them.

Araceli shook her head at Henry. She grabbed hold of Chon and put her head on his chest. She nuzzled her mouth and nose in the crook of his neck. She breathed out a long, slow breath, and Chon felt peace like he hadn't known in town, maybe never would. They were technically nowhere—half Greenton, half Falfurrias.

She looked up at him. "How was work?"

"Started off shitty, but ended great." Chon had never answered this question from Araceli with anything but it sucked. She leaned back, interested.

"Why?"

"I quit."

"What?" she said.

"You quit?" Henry shouted. "Bullshit. You are a liar and a scoundrel and a piece of shit who is trying to make some kind of stupid joke."

Henry's audience hooted and hollered.

"Ana quit this morning. So it was just me and Rocha. He called the owner, complaining that he wouldn't have anyone to relieve him tomorrow. So I get a call from San Antonio near the end of my shift. He says there's nothing we can do. I have to work, have to miss graduation. So I told him I'd stock the cooler, clean the store, and put my key in the mail slot after I locked up."

Chon was only talking to Araceli. He looked over at Henry who was hanging on his every word too. The entire crowd around the Suburban had hushed and were straining to hear Chon's story over the sounds of the partiers around the circle who didn't know Chon had a story worth shutting up to hear. When he finished talking, he scanned Araceli's eyes, looking for her thoughts on his decision. It was probably the booze, but Araceli didn't seem to have caught up to what Chon said.

"Well, you know what? Fuck Artie Alba," she finally said.

"Yeah," Henry said quietly and without the slightest slur. Then he shouted again. "Fuck him!"

Everyone laughed. Henry was fired up by his audience. He looked at Chon and smiled. "You know what? Come here."

But Henry didn't wait. He charged at Chon like a bull. Chon turned heel to run. It was too late. Henry grabbed him from behind. Chon's first instinct was to fight. To throw an elbow behind himself or to turn around and swing a fist, but this was Henry, so he didn't.

Henry grabbed frantically at Chon's shirt, that stupid shirt he wore to work. Araceli pleaded with her cousin to let go of Chon. The crowd around them began cheering and laughing. Henry got a hand under the buttons of Chon's shirt. He tugged it back, breaking them all off.

Chon was starting to get angry. He turned around, chest exposed, ready to hit Henry, but a former football player joined the scuffle. He grabbed Chon's arms so Henry could strip Chon of his shirt. Once he got it, he raised it above his head triumphantly. Chon fought and squirmed to get at Henry.

"Ya, calmate, bro. He's just having a good time," the drunken linebacker said. He loosened his grip and Chon calmed down. The linebacker kept his arms loosely around Chon, like they were spooning standing up. They watched Henry.

"Fuck Artie Alba. Fuck the Pachanga, and fuck Greenton," Henry said.

The audience cheered and laughed, but Henry wasn't laughing anymore. He looked, clear-eyed and calm, at Chon.

"You're not his fucking slave anymore. You're your own man. The world is yours, brother. Fuck this."

He walked over to the fire and threw the shirt on it. At this point, everyone out at the ranch that night who hadn't stolen away with a lover or passed out drunk on the bed of a truck was watching Henry. They hollered chaotically at the sight of destruction and what they thought was sure to turn to a fight. Henry walked back from the fire smiling at Chon expectantly, like he was waiting for his best friend to get in on the joke. He didn't know if it was because of Henry's smile or because of his having set the shirt on fire, but Chon started laughing. The linebacker who was holding him laughed too, gave Chon a slap on the chest and let him go.

Henry held his hands palm-up at his side. He was breathing heavily from the excitement. He had gotten so close to the fire that there were black stains under his nose where he'd been breathing in smoke. "Fuck it, right?" he said to Chon. Not even Araceli heard him.

"Yeah, fuck it. You idiot, I have nine more shirts like that at home."

Araceli did hear this, and she laughed. Chon laughed too. Henry joined them. They were there at the center of most of Greenton High's student body, laughing together, Chon and Araceli falling into each other's arms, Henry coming up and giving them a big bear hug.

The party wore on. Chon had a few drinks, but saw there was no point in trying to catch up with Henry and Araceli or with anyone for that matter. He decided to just relax and watch the party fall apart around him. People were swaying and tripping and throwing up drunk. Boyfriends and girlfriends were fighting over what Chon could only hear to be nonsense. At close to three in the morning, Chon told Araceli and Henry it was time to go. The fire had died out. The place had degenerated to a bunch of walking, talking unmet hormonal needs and desires. Between Henry and Araceli, Henry was the better of the two to drive the Suburban the four miles to Araceli's house.

"I want to ride with Chon," Araceli said.

"Alright," he told her, putting his arm down around her back to even out her crooked walk and help her navigate the loose, craggy soil they had to cross over to get to the Dodge-nasty. "But you have to ride in the back seat."

"Oh, Chon, you're so dirty." She laughed and threw her head back, making her that much harder to handle.

"I'm serious. The seatbelt doesn't work on the passenger seat and if I get seen with you sitting there we might get pulled over...or I might die." Chon said the last part under his breath.

"Okay," she said. "But you have to warm me up first. It's cold."

"You're cold? I'm the one without a shirt."

When they got to the car, Araceli propped herself up and sat on the hood while Chon cleared a spot on his cluttered back seat for her. When there was enough room, he met her up at the hood. She wrapped her legs around his waist and pulled him to her. She rubbed his cold arms.

"So what are you going to do?" she asked. "You quit your job. That's huge. What's next?"

And then, looking at Araceli in the moonlight, Chon declared to be his plan what had only fleetingly entered his mind on the way over to the ranch.

"I think I'm moving up to Austin. If you think that's a good idea."

"That sounds perfect." Araceli dug her face into Chon's chest. "That's what I've been hoping for. I was just afraid to ask you to quit your job and leave your family, leave town. It seemed too huge for me to ask you to do after only a few months. But I just...I love you so much."

"I love you too. Besides, with you gone, what would I do in this town but work and get stupid?"

Chon pushed Araceli's shoulders back gently so he could look her in the face to see if it registered anything more than her words were telling him. She seemed happy, genuinely happy, like she might need Chon as much as he needed her. She tightened her legs' squeeze on Chon's waist. They kissed.

"What is this shit? Are you fucking her right here for everyone to see," someone shouted.

Chon turned around smiling, expecting to see Henry coming toward them, but it wasn't Henry. It was someone taller and skinnier than Henry—not as tall as Chon, but harder looking. He was approaching quickly. Two other boys were at his heels. Chon strained his eyes to make out who it was but he couldn't see for the shine of headlights behind him. When his eyes adjusted as much as they were going to, he still couldn't tell who was heading toward them, but he could definitely see that the guy was carrying a stick of some sort.

Chon picked Araceli up from the car, carried her almost like a toddler, her legs still straddling him. He ran her around to the other side of the Dodge-nasty, putting her down quickly but gently. He looked over in the direction of the cars to see if he could make out Henry, hoping there was help on the way, but there wasn't. There were only three guys, and one of them was carrying what Chon could now see was a baseball bat.

That guy got to the back of the Dodge-nasty. He tapped the trunk three times, as if it were home plate. One of the boys with him said, "Batter up."

He pulled the bat back and gracefully—with so much force being culled from so little effort, like a swing that looks like a slap bunt but carries to the left field wall—smashed in the car's rear window. Araceli screamed. Chon pushed her back a step.

The guy with the bat swung down on the trunk a few times. He walked around behind the car and gave the right back panel a swift chop, like he was trying to hit a ball that had broken just below the strike zone. He turned to face Chon. He pointed the bat at Chon, calling his shot. Araceli screamed again.

People rushed over from the party to see what was happening. The guy with the bat, someone who Chon now saw to be baby-faced—not old enough to be a senior—opened his batting stance and rolled his wrists, cutting a circle in the air in front of him.

"Domingo?" Araceli said. "What's wrong with you? What do you think you're doing?"

"What's wrong with you, goddamnit? You're the one who's here with him. Making out and hanging all over him in front of everyone like John never existed."

A crowd surrounded Chon, Araceli and Domingo. Chon relaxed at little. Because no matter how much they wanted a show, people wouldn't stand around and watch someone get beaten to death by a freshman-turned-sophomore wielding a bat—even if he batted .400 and led the district in RBI.

"Are you fucking serious? I'm supposed to die because John did? I'm not supposed to graduate or move on or fall in love with someone else?" Araceli was shouting, angry tears running down the sides of her face. Domingo shook his head.

"But him? This guy?" Domingo said, still in his batting stance, wagging the bat back and forth in front of him.

"What? I should be with you? Because you're the best player on the team you get to inherit me? Just because you can swing a bat doesn't mean you're not an asshole."

"Listen, bitch—" Domingo said, shaking his head like he was trying to not lose his temper with a lady.

"Hey!" Chon shouted. "You don't talk to her like that."

Domingo looked at Chon there in front of him, shirtless and ready to fight. The sight seemed to remind him of why he had grabbed the bat to begin with.

"So what? You waited for him to die so you could be with her? I bet you wished for him to die. You fucking prayed for him to die so you could get into her pants." Domingo rolled his wrists faster, making a whooshing sound that Chon could hear from where he stood.

"What I pray about is between me and God. But I will say that if John had never died, I would never have gotten with her. She's the best thing that's ever happened to me. So you do the math on that. But if I had the power to change the past, I'd make him live."

"But you can't, can you? You can't change the past. You just benefit from it," Domingo said.

"If you're going to beat my head in with a baseball bat because of that, you have a lot of people here who you have to beat up. So why don't you do us a favor and start with yourself."

The look in Domingo's eyes got crazy. He stepped forward. Chon stepped up too.

Araceli pulled his shoulder, but Chon shrugged her off. If he was going to be beaten with a baseball bat, he was going to make himself a moving, swinging target.

Chon's words and the psychotic, murderous look on Domingo's face sobered up enough people in the crowd for them to step between the boys and stop what would have been an ugly fight. Domingo's own partners in crime, the ones who had walked over with him and goaded him on, restrained him and took away his baseball bat. They pulled him screaming and crying to their car and drove off. Everyone else stared at Chon. He didn't give the slightest of damns what they thought about him.

He went back to Araceli. She was shaking.

"I'm so sorry," he said. "I had to make sure he didn't hurt you."

Araceli shook her head. "Goddamn, we need to get out of this town," she said.

Chon wrapped his arms around her and held her until she calmed down. As the crowd of people around the Dodge-nasty dispersed, each of them walking behind the car, appraising the damage Domingo had done, Henry made his way over from the circle.

"And where the fuck were you?" Araceli said.

"Marie Canales," he said, pointing a thumb behind him.

Marie was one of Araceli's former cheerleader friends, the duchess for every dance court over which Araceli presided as queen. Henry stood there, flush of face, breathing heavily. Seeing his concern, measuring the magnitude of a score of Marie Canales' proportions, Chon had to stifle a laugh.

"This is serious," Araceli said.

"What is?" Henry said.

She looked at him, said, "Oh damn it, Henry."

Henry looked around, confused. He finally saw what had been done to the Dodge-nasty.

189

"Holy shit, who did this?"

"Domingo Talamantes," Chon said.

"The baseball player? Is that motherfucker still here? Let's go get his ass."

Araceli told Henry that he had been dragged away and driven into town. Henry started screaming and cursing. Chon was glad that he hadn't been there for what went down. If he had been, one or both of them would have gotten baseball bat-sized dents in the sides of their faces.

When he finally calmed down, Henry admitted, "You know what, I'm glad I was where I was. You survived. And did I mention Marie Canales?"

"Cochino," Araceli said. "Let's go home."

"Alright," Chon said. "But you have to ride with Henry."

The next day was graduation. The GHS band's tuba player fell off beat over and over again, making a train wreck of "Pomp and Circumstance." After the salutatorian's speech, (he mentioned disappointment at the turn of the century arriving without any of the Jetsons' 'promises,' as he called them, being fulfilled), Chon wished his parents hadn't forced him to dress up and go. After the valedictorian's (she mentioned Jesus carrying her along the shore during times when she could only see one set of footprints in the sand behind her), Chon wished only for death. Even sitting with Araceli and Henry on either side of him didn't make it better. Well, Henry made it a little better with his comments and jokes about how full of shit it all was. And how right he was!

That night, Chon and his family went over to Araceli's house for a big barbecue celebrating the graduations of two Monsevaises and one Gonzalez. They would talk about the plans the kids had for going up to Austin—leaving the next day to set Araceli up in her summer school dorm. Chon would drive in the Dodge-nasty, while Henry followed in the Dos Reyes truck, filled with all of Araceli's possessions and some of Chon's. Chon would stay with a cousin of the Monsevaises' (an ingenious plan, Araceli's parents thought) while he looked for an apartment.

The kids had talked the parents into a weekend alone, chaperoned as it would be by Henry and the Austin-based Monsevais. They had worked hard, they told their parents, in the books and in the store to make it up there and they wanted to get up there alone, then to be visited by their parents who could then dote on and criticize their living arrangements and the crazy city they had decided to move to.

That night they would all drink and eat together and share reminiscences that included the Johns' time in Greenton. This didn't bother Chon in the least. They would speak, late into the night and after many rounds, about their fears—the parents' for their children, the children's for themselves. They would get to know each other very well. They had to, they were tied to each other now. It would be a night of great fun and hidden sadnesses. It would end with teary-eyed parents remembering when.

Earlier that day, still in his graduation shirt and tie, Chon took the bruised and beaten Dodge-nasty into the Mejia auto garage in the southwest part of town and was met by Goyo, who sat up straight on his stool when he saw Chon.

Before Chon even got out of the car, Goyo was walking around behind the car.

"Now what the hell happened here?" he said.

"Batting practice," Chon said.

"This is going to be expensive, a lot of body work."

"All I need is the rear windshield and a replacement for the passenger-side seatbelt."

"So now you're Mr. Safety?" Goyo said. "Why's that? You have some new little girl you're gonna drive around town?"

"No, I'm moving. I'm taking it to Austin."

The hustler's smile that Goyo wasn't trying to hide left his face. He looked at the car again, took another walk around it. He opened up the passenger door and stuck his head in to examine the seatbelt. He came back to Chon, his eyes looking like he was trying to figure out the complicated science of resurrection.

"Okay, I'll need to get a seatbelt ratchet from the Napa. I can probably find a windshield at the dump. Tomorrow? You're leaving tomorrow and you come here today?" he said, more curious than angry.

"Well, the windshield just happened yesterday. I guess the idea to leave did too."

"You have to be kidding me."

"But it's what I want to do. I need to do it," Chon said.

Goyo looked Chon up and down and seemed to decide the kid wasn't a one hundred percent idiot.

"Alright, I'll drop you off at your house and fix the car. It shouldn't take too long, but I have things to get."

Chon nodded his agreement and opened the driver's side door to get in the car.

"Whoa, what do you think you're doing?" Goyo said.

"Aren't you taking my car to the shop?"

"Yeah, but you get the side without the seatbelt."

Chon got out and walked around the car. Goyo fired it up and pulled it out of the garage.

"Don't worry," he said. "I'm a great driver." Then he peeled out of the alley and hooked a sharp right turn onto Sigrid.

He had the car back to Chon less than three hours later. He knocked on the door to the Gonzales house. When Chon came out, he threw the keys at him.

"You're driving."

Chon got into the car. When Goyo got in, he pulled the seatbelt down and latched it. He gave it a tug and it pulled back onto his chest. Chon looked at the rear windshield behind him. It looked brand new.

"How much do I owe you?" Chon asked Goyo. He was out of the car and leaning in at the passenger window.

"Nothing," Goyo said.

Chon looked up at him in disbelief.

"My father would kick my ass if he found out I charged you. But you know what? I'll kick your ass if you don't fix the parking break when you get the chance. The store didn't have the part. You'll be safe with it like this. Right? You'll be safe?" he asked.

"Of course," Chon said.

"You know I did this for her, right?" Goyo said.

"Yeah."

"She was like a sister to me. I guess she still is."

"I know," Chon said.

"Don't forget it."

The next day, May 23, was the first anniversary of the Johns' deaths. Chon found himself sitting behind the wheel of the Dodge-nasty, its windows rolled down and the dry wind that blew offering no relief against the heat that didn't know it wasn't actually summer yet. He was parked in front of the Mejia house. He had picked up Araceli, whose bags and belongings were in the Dos Reyes truck. She had asked if he could take her to see John's family before they left.

Chon had been waiting for almost an hour in the car. Araceli had invited him in to visit the Mejias, but he declined. When Araceli walked out of the house, she was followed by a sobbing Julie Mejia. Andres gave her a strong hug, as did Goyo, who had come to be with his parents to mourn the anniversary of his brother's passing.

Araceli walked out to the car. The Mejias' eyes followed her there. Andres and Goyo gave Chon identical hard nods. Julie waved her hand big and wide next to her ear. Chon waved back. He was parked on the street, which ended as a turnabout four houses up. He drove to the end of the street. When he pulled around and passed the house again, only Julie stood there waiting to watch them pass so that she could wave and cry some more when they drove out of sight.

They were set to meet Henry at Bryan's Stop 'n' Shop, the Pachanga's number one competitor. They had time before they had to arrive. Chon drove to the park in the center of town. The swimming pool would open for the first time all summer the next day. Kids were waiting eagerly, biding their time playing and loitering at the park. Chon drove to a far end of the park where there was a backstop set up and a team of pre-teens practicing baseball. He and Araceli got out of the car and said their goodbyes to his parents. They were able to watch one of Pito's at-bats. He watched the first pitch, a high, fat fastball that even Chon in his baseball days would not have been able to resist. When the second pitch came at him, Pito pulled around a compact, efficient swing. The ball was launched far out into the deep recesses of the park. If this were a game, it certainly would have cleared the Little League fence, probably the high school one too. But there was no fence, and the outfielder was chasing the ball like mad. Still, Pito rounded the bases at a slow, steady trot. He was getting practice for all of the home runs he would surely be hitting during summer league and beyond.

Chon and Araceli cheered, shouting and screaming and embarrassing Pito. They went over to him at the side of the imaginary diamond.

"Chon, I'm playing," he said.

"No you're not, you're practicing."

"Same thing."

"Yeah, you're right. But hey, we're leaving. I want you to be good and play hard, okay? When school starts, your grades better stay where they were all this last year," Chon said.

Chon had never spoken to his brother like this. He had given advice when it was asked for, but never took the tone of someone with any authority on anything. It felt weird, but it felt right. Pito seemed to think so too, because he said, "Alright, Chon. Don't worry."

"Good," Chon said.

Araceli gave Pito a hug, and Chon gave him a handshake.

"Drive safe," Pito shouted at them as they walked away.

They filled up at Bryan's (Araceli paid). Chon went over the plan with Henry. They would take 16 to San Antonio. When they got there, they would take the 410 loop to 35 and then north to Austin. If they needed to stop, they could call each other. Araceli's mom made her take her cell phone, and Henry had the Dos Reyes company cell.

"Okay, Magellan, let's just fucking go," Henry said. And so they did.

Driving up Main, which was Highway 16, they passed by the east end of the high school. Out his window, Chon could see that there was a ceremony, slapdash and unofficial-looking. People held flowers in their hands and Mr. Adame was standing in front of the assembled, probably speaking absolute nonsense. They drove on. With Greenton behind them, Araceli grabbed Chon's hand. They had made it out. If it all fell apart and they had to come back in a week, they would always have left.

She looked over at him and shouted over the sound of wind rushing in through the rolled-down windows. "I love you."

"I love you too," Chon said. He didn't bother to shout. He couldn't. He was using everything he had to resist the urge to break down at the thought of leaving everything he had ever known in the orange-red dust behind him. Araceli smiled at the words she read on his lips.

Chon wondered when the landscape around them would change. He wondered if they would be able to roll up the windows as the temperatures dropped more the farther north they went. He thought of the cool he was driving toward and was happy that it would offer him and Araceli peace from the howling wind that made talking impossible. The future seemed endless. Not knowing what it held scared Chon like he couldn't say, but it had to be better than what they were leaving. Of course it would be better. He pushed down on the accelerator, leaned over the center console, and kissed Araceli, the girl of his dreams.

The first anniversary memorial of the Johns' dying was the last formal event that would be held in town to honor the Johns, save for the priest at church blessing their eternal souls and a room full of worshippers asking for the Lord to hear their prayers on the Sunday of every anniversary week to come.

This is not to say that the boys would be forgotten. At Flojos, there will be occasional effusive toasts to the Johns from that day forward until there is no one left in town who even knew them or who could remember any word of them. Still, at Little League games, fathers—standing around the tailgates of trucks pulled around back of the centerfield fence—will crack beers and talk tall about how this boy or that boy—or, if they were so blessed, *their* boy—might just have the stuff to be Greenton's next John.

In time, town will no longer mourn the boys. They will no longer be a wound that fate dealt Greenton. There will barely be a scar left to remind people of their passing.

Their numbers will still be on the uniforms of the baseball and football teams. Coach Gallegos will still have each of his players touch the plaques that hung at the baseball stadium's entrance before leading them onto the diamond for the first game of the season. Yet the Johns' impression on the athletes of Greenton will fade. As each new season starts, the boys will remember less and less of the baseball gods made flesh and bone. Eventually, all they will have will be memories of a happening they were too young to understand—the tears, the craziness of everyone around them, the concept of death itself. Then, one day the Greyhound baseball team will be made up of a squad of boys who have no worldly recollection of the Johns or even of the spectacle that was made of their dying. They will see the plaques at the stadium and the jerseys that hang framed outside the main office as just another bit of visual white noise, like so many inspirational posters in classrooms and throughout school. They will be passed by, unnoticed by everyone but the occasional nostalgic teacher and the janitors, who will be charged with Windexing them and wiping them clean to near invisibility.

All of this was just fine with the Mejias, who had stopped taking part in everything that was made of the passing of their son and his best friend. With two boys buried, their public mourning was done. It was back to business as usual, at least for Andres and Goyo. Julie could never bring herself to return to work at the library. She was never fired. They just stopped cutting checks to her, reassuring her every now and then that her job was waiting for her when she was ready to return to it, but she never readied herself for that return.

When she died, almost two years after the Johns, it brought a spark of life back to the story of the Johns. She had been diagnosed with bone cancer that February. She was dead within four months. As went the town's thinking—their contextual read on the real life happenings they watched like a soap opera—she gave up. With John gone—they thought and told each other—she had nothing to fight for. She wanted to be with her boy, and so she let go.

Not only was this line of thinking wrong, it was unfair. It was unfair to Andres and Goyo, who the people of town seemed to be saying weren't worth fighting for as much as John. It was unfair to Julie, who fought as hard as she could for as long as she could, and who suffered a painful fight, whose inevitable end she was ashamed to tearfully tell her husband and son she was afraid of.

But people will have their stories. They'll have their gossip and their assumptions without any regard or compassion for those they are watching, because why should something as pesky as caring get in the way of what is genuine entertainment?

Just shy of their own end, Chon and Araceli returned to town together for Julia's funeral. Araceli cried with Andres—held his hand throughout the whole ceremony. Chon sat by her side, patting her shoulder and wiping her tears. Goyo, on the other side of his father, did not play the tough guy he had played at his brother's funeral, instead taking up his own hyena cackle at the loss of his mother.

Arn and Angie Robison came back to Greenton for the funeral. Though they were in a different car, when the royal blue Cadillac coupe rolled into town, everyone who saw it knew it was them. The plot thickened. Without the death at the center of it all being marked as inordinately tragic or unexpected or devastating—it was just cancer, just a middle-aged woman, not two boys on their way to glory—no one in town felt the need to check their gossip, to hide their widened eyes or pretend to not be eavesdropping at the funeral. They were spectators, shameless and crazy for action.

Lost in their thoughts of the woman they lost, Andres and Goyo seemed thankfully oblivious to the fire behind the eyes of their neighbors, but Chon could see it, and it disgusted him. When they came around to pay their condolences to the bereaved, Chon could see that the Robisons were disgusted by it too. He could have gone back to the Mejia house after the funeral to hear their thoughts on the subject over menudo made by Araceli's mom, but he asked Araceli to drop him at his parents' house instead. He told her he would go if she needed him, but otherwise, it was a time for family, and he wasn't that.

By then, all of the John stars had faded and been removed from the cars they adorned. Even Ms. Salinas had taken the last one off her car. The green on the uniforms bought by the money the stars made was also getting dull with so much washing and grass and red dirt stains. At home, Chon had dinner with his parents, who didn't much care to join everyone else in town at a funeral, and his brother, who hoped, in two years, to be wearing one of those jerseys. His parents asked Chon about work and school and how he and Araceli were doing. It was quiet and peaceful, and Chon was glad he hadn't gone with Araceli to the Mejia house.

At the Mejia's, the Robisons expressed their sincere and heartfelt condolences. They had lost a friend in Julie, one who, like the rest of their world, they had really lost when the Johns died. They shared in the storytelling and remembering. They laughed at the funny stories and cried at the sad ones. Arn had bought a bottle of the same expensive bourbon he always drank, the kind he had shared with the Mejias in celebration of their boys having made it.

It was during a lull in the sad festivities that Arn addressed an issue that Andres knew had to be brought up at some point or other. The Robisions were there for him, for Julie, and so Andres did not begrudge Arn bringing up the last of the dirty business that remained in the wake of the boys dying.

What were they going to do to Ford and to Firestone and to all of the other bastards who had made the cars and tires that had a hand in killing their boys?

Arn and Angie had been in contact with their family attorney. He told them the way to go was class action. These accidents were happening all over the country and the companies could no longer hide from the truth or deny blame. There was a big lawsuit being put together, and Arn was going to be damned if his boy's name wasn't going to be on the list of those killed by negligence and greed and poor engineering.

They needed to pay, he told Andres, and not just money.

Andres agreed. He didn't want a lawyer. He didn't want to testify. He didn't want anything but to sign papers and be done with it. Arn said he would have his attorney arrange everything, and he did.

When the payout came, Andres had few wants that could be met by money. He paid off his home and truck, he paid off Goyo's too. He gave Goyo most of what was left and, in turn, Goyo made it his duty to pull Andres out of himself, to get him out of the house and, on occasion, out of Greenton. Andres made his way to Houston pretty often to see the Astros and eventually the Texans. Every time he did, he would visit the Robisons. He would never dream of putting them out by asking to stay with them, but there was always dinner and a few drinks to be shared with old friends.

One year, he had Goyo take him to Corpus Christi to see the Islanders of the university there play baseball against UT. The boys in burnt orange looked bigger, stronger, of a different pedigree than the Corpus team. They won by thirteen runs. Though he never told Goyo, Andres felt it was a personal victory that he did not cry at the sight of all of that youth and power and perfection—athletic and otherwise.

On the night of Julie Mejia's funeral, Henry came by in a big black dooly truck with running lights on the roof and Tres Reyes Welding Works written on the doors. They drove around town silently. They parked by the cemetery, vacated and looking like there hadn't been a funeral that day.

"How's she doing?" Henry asked. He was talking a lot less these days. It would take at least five beers before he got going.

"She's okay," Chon said. "She went to the house with all of them to have menudo and share memories and all that. I didn't feel like it was my place."

Henry nodded. He looked tired, old. He had gained weight and put on such a fierce tan that he looked like someone else.

"And you, how are you doing?" Chon asked.

"I'm good," he said. "Working."

Chon nodded. Henry reached behind the seat and pulled a couple of beers from the case he had on the floorboard. Chon grabbed one. Henry held firm to it.

"These are mine," he said, cracking one and taking a drink.

Chon looked for a sign that his friend was joking. When none came, he turned around to grab a beer. Henry reached over and handed Chon one of the beers.

"I'm fucking with you, man. I'm just fucking with you."

Chon laughed, opened the beer he'd been given, and took a drink.

"Crazy day?" Henry asked.

"I can remember crazier," Chon said. "It did piss me off the way they all acted, like the funeral was all a show, her dying. I just hoped the Mejias didn't notice."

"They did," Henry said. "But they won't realize it until later and even then they won't be too pissed."

Chon looked at the man who he had counted as his best friend throughout their shared childhood. He was a different person, changed by a life in a welding rig with his father and uncle. He was hard now. Still round, but hard. Chon looked at the grass in the ditch out his window.

"You still come see your mom?" he asked.

"Not as much as I should," Henry said.

"Do you want to go now?"

"No," Henry said. "Not just now."

He turned the truck's radio on and a conjunto song filled the emptiness in the cab. He opened another beer and took a long pull that turned into something of a passionate kiss between himself and the drink. When he pulled the can away, he crushed it in his hand and gave a long belch.

Chon couldn't help but laugh.

"What in the world did you eat today?" he asked. "That smells awful." He opened his door.

"Now I'm ready," Henry said.

He grabbed some beers from the pack, then walked around the back of the truck. Together he and Chon broke into the cemetery to pay their respects to the dead of Greenton, TX.

2002

Chon rubbed his arms against a cool breeze that blew on downtown Austin in late August. He thumbed a cigarette from the pack he had in the breast pocket of his shirt. Kamel Reds. He'd drunkenly picked a box of them off a shelf behind a bar a year ago and kept buying them when he woke up hung-over the next morning and found he liked how they tasted.

Cigarettes were something he picked up in Austin. Going to bars and parties, he smoked with people around him over conversations soul-baring and full of shit. But cigarettes weren't Chon. Much of the way he was living then wasn't either. Chon didn't know who he was or who he wanted to be, but he knew that much.

He stood alone on line on Lavaca outside of Antone's, a bar that started as a blues joint but now housed alternative and hip-hop bands too. It was Jimmie Vaughn on a Thursday, Blue October that Friday, and Talib Kweli on Saturday. Antone's was an old Austin establishment, a microcosm of the whole city—a rocking metaphor for how the whole place seemed to run. His friends hadn't wanted to wait in line with him or to pay the concert cover charge, so they said they'd meet up with him over on Sixth.

Chon flashed his fake I.D. at a bouncer who seemed more interested in the fashion choices of the young ladies waiting to get in than whether or not a kid one month away from drinking legally was actually named Lester Maxwell, DOB 12/16/1980. Chon wasn't in the mood for drinking, but it cut three dollars off his cover. The big room was already packed. The air was thick with sweat and smoke and the products people used to make themselves seem more beautiful than they were. Chon staked out a spot for himself in front of stage right.

A while after the opening band finished their set, as the members of the band wrapped cords the lengths of their forearms around their elbows and in their palms and carried amplifiers and encased guitars from the stage, a security guy gave Chon a harsh nudge with his shoulder and told him to make way. He was escorting the main act's girlfriend—a woman who looked much smaller than you imagine her to be when you see her in the movies—up to the VIP section in a loft above the crowd. There was something about that exchange that made Chon happy. He was miles and miles away from Greenton, and just one very big degree of separation away from America's sweetheart. It made Chon wish someone were there to tell this to.

The next time Henry came to town, Chon thought, they would go to Antone's. They would listen to whoever was playing, have a few beers. And they would try to fill somehow the gaps that months apart and different lifestyles had put between them.

Next to Chon, a couple of people were pointing at a lanky, ridiculous-looking man in a tight black T-shirt and leather pants. There he stood, a few people in front of Chon, the daytime Hollywood actor and nighttime aspiring blues singer whose band would be headlining the next night's show at Antone's to about a quarter of the place's capacity. Chon noticed, but didn't say anything. The thing in a situation like this was to not say anything. The people next to Chon did not seem to know this.

"Hey, look," one of the guys said loud enough to be heard on stage. "It's [insert movie star/blues singer's more famous older brother's name]."

The low lights and smoke-filled air couldn't hide the shades of red the actor's face turned. He was done slumming it with the commoners on the floor. He walked over to the VIP door and headed upstairs where people knew how to blow smoke for a man in leather pants. Chon laughed.

The crowd moved up a spot into the sinkhole forming, person by person, in the space the actor had vacated. The music hadn't started so things weren't packed yet. Chon looked around at all the cool people wearing their fashion like their lives depended on it, and all the hip people their unfashion like nothing had ever depended on anything. Chon didn't count himself one of them, but this was mainly because he felt he would never be cool. He would never be hip. He would never be Austin.

He wanted to believe that in the three years he had been gone from Greenton, he had shed more of the place than his melodic country-Spanglish drawl—he was still bringing words cadentially upward to sarcastic-sounding blue notes, making his statements sound like questions, but now he wasn't doing it after every sentence.

But his ties to home were ones that almost couldn't be identified and, as such, were harder to break than changing the way he spoke. No one he met could even point to Greenton on a map, much less look at him, listen to him, get to know him and say that that was where he came from, that Greenton had made Chon Gonzales.

But the place *had* made Chon. It was hard enough living alone at twenty in a city of strangers, but to have no one to share his frame of reference—as he had with almost everyone in Greenton—was lonelier than the efficiency apartment he called home on the far east end of Stassney. He'd made friends at work, some at school. He even knew a guy from Benavides he figured he might have met at some high school function or other. Chon probably never would have crossed paths with the guy in Austin except Chon was wearing a Greenton High School shirt in class one day and the guy sparked up a conversation for no other reason than that they were both from such similar places and both likely feeling the same brand of loneliness.

Chon never thought he would have to face the city alone. And, really, he didn't have to. He could always call Araceli. He knew she would drop whatever she was doing and listen, just like he would, to someone who knew the same street names and nicknames and tall tales and histories she did. He knew she would help him because she loved him.

Now Chon understood that it had been foolish to ever think that there could be a forever between the two of them, even if they did leave home together. They had to meet new people, encounter new cultures, experience the world. Chon had never seen an Asian person in the flesh, never met anyone from a different continent other than the South Americans who had begun making their way across the border looking for food and water when they got into town on their way to Chicago or Michigan or anywhere else they had family getting started on the dream. It was almost sure to be too much for them.

Here it was, the final proof that what he was trying to outrun wasn't Greenton or what it had made of him, but an embarrassing adolescence he had just barely escaped: he was in a crowded bar in the middle of downtown Austin, and all he could think about was Araceli Monsevais. It wasn't thankless, unwarranted pining anymore. They shared a history together, all of history. Everyone reminisces fondly and regretfully about their lost loves. Chon knew there was no shame in his thoughts. But it was the act of longing, the awakening of those avenues in his brain or of those muscles in his soul, that took him back to a time that filled him with such shame that no amount of new friends or growing up could make that shame sting any less. Chon never caught wise to the fact that he wasn't the only person who had times and past lives to look back on in horror. But that was always his failing, thinking he was the only one.

Now, with the room near full and getting crazy—his mind swimming in the thoughts that being alone in a city full of people always brought—Chon wanted a beer. He abandoned his spot in the crowd to get to the bar. It was no real loss. Skinny as he still was, he could elbow and sidestep his way back up to a prime piece of floor when the show started.

Chon ordered. The bartender gave him the first longneck she could reach in the trough in front of her. Chon had no objection to the brand she'd pulled. As he turned to walk away, someone tapped him on the shoulder. Before he could look to see who it was, Araceli grabbed the scruff of hair behind his right ear like she always did when she walked into the kitchen of his apartment after class and he was at the stove, cooking their dinner.

This happened more than Chon would have thought it would. He'd be walking on campus or around downtown or on the trail at Lake Austin, thinking of home and of Araceli and of better times when he'd had her, and she would pop up, just like that. It wasn't as unlikely an occurrence as he thought it to be. Austin is a very small city. It's easy to spot someone in a crowd when they're the only person in the world you're ever looking for.

He turned around, smiling. She pulled him in for a tight, quick, excited hug, then kissed him on the cheek. It was a small, tender kiss. Chon wished he had turned his face the fifteen degrees it would take for their lips to meet, but that would have complicated the serendipitous turn that brought her to Antone's.

"What are you doing here?" she asked.

"Supporting our boy. Major label record release party, Bob's gone big time."

"Can you believe it—our CD, in Best Buys and Wal-Marts all over the country?" She flicked at the bottle in Chon's hand. "Your birthday come early this year?"

"Door was cheaper for 21 and up," Chon said.

"Yeah, and you just paid the difference with that beer." Her tone was playful, that great Monsevais humor that Chon had come to hate in Araceli because it could so easily be turned passive-aggressive and actively cruel. But she was there, smiling at Chon, with the red and blue and white lights from the truss above the stage making more cruel the fact that she hadn't gone there with him.

"You look really great tonight," Chon said.

"Don't change the subject."

"Oh, I'm sorry. What were we talking about?"

"Nothing," she said. "Anything but how great I look."

Chon nodded and looked away. For as much as it stung to be there with her but not with her, Chon was reminded of the reason they hadn't worked.

"Alright," Chon said. She looked at him with a sort of desperation on her face, like he was about to walk away from her and out of the bar. He remembered that look and hated himself for ever hurting her. "I look great tonight."

Araceli laughed. "You do."

"Wow, really believable," Chon said.

She put her hand on his collarbone. "You really do."

"Ladies and gentlemen," the call came on the speakers, "Bob Schneider and Lonelyland."

The band took the stage. The Mexican-looking guy behind the drum set clicked a four count and away they went. The bass player—tall, near albino—played an electric upright and danced around his three square feet of stage. Behind him, a three-piece horn section played swells and fills to the music. In front of where Chon had been standing before he left to get a drink, an older man sat on stage with a cello between his legs. Bob Schneider took the stage carrying an electric guitar with dice in place of the volume and tone knobs. He thanked the audience for coming out and started playing.

"Let's get closer," Araceli shouted. She grabbed Chon's hand and pulled him into the crowd that separated them from the stage.

Whereas he would have had to advance his way to the stage forcefully, Araceli did it gracefully—making eye contact with the people she was cutting off and making eyes at the space that wasn't really in front of them. They all moved, even the women, and Chon remembered what it was like walking into a place with Araceli.

They ended up near the front of the crowd in the center of the audience.

It wasn't Austin that had come between Chon and Araceli. It wasn't moving into a world so shiny and dirty and well-lit.

There were two things that did Chon and Araceli in. One was that she was too beautiful for Chon to let out into a world where he had everyone pegged as schemers and thieves—out to take from him what he had been working all these last years to get. It was that and the fact that Chon couldn't sack up the confidence to trick himself into believing that he deserved Araceli or—he would realize years later—happiness either. Defining himself by his pursuit of something he didn't believe he was worthy of for so long had taken its toll on Chon. He shuddered to think of what his life would have been like if he hadn't gotten Araceli. But if he hadn't gotten her, he believed he probably would have lived through her moving out of town to join the boyfriend who would hypothetically not have died. Chon thought he might even have moved to Austin on his own to live the life of a satisfied, well-adjusted man one month shy of his 21st birthday, as though such people really existed. Realistically, though, he knew he most likely would still be manning the register at the Pachanga if it weren't for her.

He didn't trust the men she saw and encountered and almost surely flirted with on campus when she was going to school and he was working. Then, when he started school a semester after she did, he didn't trust the men who were in classes with her when he wasn't. Then he didn't trust the women she had begun hanging out with in the honor sorority she'd joined. He held on tight, too tight, to what he really believed was being stolen from him. He felt undermined by the world around him. It was all out to get her. It was all a valid option for Araceli and a threat to Chon's whole world.

When they moved to Austin, Chon got a small apartment in West Campus to be close to Araceli. She didn't spend more than a handful of nights in her dorm that first semester. Initially, each of them felt they were the picture of domestic bliss, like they were something more than two children playing house. But Araceli made friends and joined groups and went to parties without Chon, who often had to work night shifts at a gas station where he'd gotten a job. He knew it wasn't fair to expect her to stay home and wait for her boyfriend to come back stinking of busted beer bottles and stale coffee. But he had in his head the certitude, the unshakeable certitude, that she would one day be stolen from him, that he would be left alone in a cold and isolating city by the only person he knew there.

That made him get angry when she came home late. There were shouting matches that he felt didn't end well. They made her cry. She started going back to her dorm room after nights of partying. Then he flung accusations at her. One night it was all too much.

He went out with a co-worker after work. He picked up a girl and took her back to his apartment. Araceli came home that night, and it was all over. She told him she would never forgive him. He decided this was not only fair, but just—as right as things get.

When she left, he realized that he hadn't had it in him to hurt the queen of his adult life. And he didn't want to hurt her, but he had to do something with their relationship. So what he did was load a gun and rest it gently on the temple of all they had together. He pulled the trigger on them, not on her. He did it because he couldn't

SEEING OFF THE JOHNS

stand wondering, worrying, dreading when the hammer would fall. It was an act of cowardice and self-preservation—Araceli was collateral damage.

She slammed the door. Chon politely asked the girl he'd brought home to leave. He fell to the ground crying before she even gathered her things. He wept and pounded the floor and pounded his chest and cursed himself, sobbing, to sleep. He woke in the morning with a throbbing pain behind his eyes. On his phone, he had seven missed calls from Henry.

That was in the summer before their second year of college. Their relationship hadn't lasted two years. She came over and got her things and asked Chon for an explanation. He had nothing to say. It required more honesty of him than he was ready or able to give. He apologized. She punched him in the face and asked him please to stay out of her life.

Araceli stood in front of Chon in the tight crowd. What could he do with his hands? He could raise them up in a flail-dance, Michael Stipe sort of way, but he couldn't do that. He couldn't further obscure the view of those behind him. He was already too tall.

It would have been natural to move his hands up into Araceli's personal space, as one tends to do with the only person they know in a crowd, former lovers or not. That didn't feel right either. He kept them at his sides, standing in an awkward Frankenstein stance that he figured was just one of many punishments he would suffer in life for having let Araceli go.

This song or that would start, and Araceli would look up over her shoulder at Chon behind her and smile. During a song about drinking and lying to someone, she looked up as if to shame him, but in a way that indicated parts of their past had stopped hurting. When a song they had listened to with Henry, prompting him to call it, "Hippy, faggy, Austin shit," was played, it made them both laugh, and she slapped at his lap behind her. Then the opening chords for a song, their song, made her turn full around and look up at Chon, who couldn't help but to smile. She wrapped her arms around the small of his back and rested her face on his chest like she used to do in the fifteen-minute increments that would pass between a morning's alarm clock sounding and its snooze-bar re-up.

Chon grabbed her in his arms and held her tight, like if he let go she would fall away from him forever. For just the under-three minutes of song time, the two of them had never hurt each other. They had never left Greenton. They were back home, parked in back of the Pachanga, dancing to Araceli's dad's Suburban playing the tune they decided then to be theirs. On stage, the cellist gave the song a somber undertone and Bob Schneider sang about the world exploding into love all around him, but Chon and Araceli didn't see any of it because they were dancing with their eyes closed.

The song's end brought them back. Bob Schneider made small talk with the audience while tuning his guitar. Araceli looked up at Chon with regret no longer borne of anger, but now of disappointment. How could you have this and build it into something beautiful, and then squander it and tear it all down? She gave Chon the lightest of slaps on the face, but her hand lingered and he wanted to fall into it, out of Austin and out of the reality he had made for them.

"So," Schneider said from the stage. Araceli turned around to face the show. "I recorded this song we're about to play in 1998, as a kind of hypothetical thing. Like, in 2002, I'll have fucked everything up and I'll write you this letter catching up with you." He pointed a hand toward the audience, making everyone the recipient of his hypothetical letter. "But now, it is 2002, and I realize that there will be people in every audience I play it for who think that I had to write an actual letter, and that the song is about something different than it is." He said the last part in a funny, mock-frustrated voice. The audience laughed. "Oh well," he said. "You'll know. Austin'll know."

Then he sang the words, "The year's 2002. I'm doing exactly what I wanted to."

The song he sang had always come off as pretty brilliant, although too twangy for Chon's taste. But tonight it was an indictment of him. It was a prophesy, foretold in the speakers of Araceli's father's truck, on the independent release of the album, fulfilled here at Antone's three years after the fact. Chon listened to the words of the song—catching up with an old love, recapping a personal downfall, revealing that the narrator's not okay—and they had an effect on him that made him shed himself for a minute. He wrapped his arms around Araceli at her shoulders and crossed them in front of her. As the song played on, Chon could feel tears falling from her face onto his bare arms, them, along with the words of the song, serving as a welcome kind of torture, a purgative burning, one that didn't absolve Chon of all he'd done wrong but made him feel cleaner in his guilt than he'd felt in close to two years.

The band played a three-hour set. After the show, Chon waited for Araceli to use the restroom and walked her out to the street.

"That was so much fun," she said. "I can't believe they played that long."

"I know," Chon said. "I'm tired, I can only imagine how they're feeling."

Araceli pulled a phone from her pocket and looked at its backlit display.

"Whoa," she said. "It's late."

"I know. I'm starving. Do you want to go get food?"

"I would—" she started, but Chon cut her off.

"Hey, it's fine. I totally get it. It's later than I thought it would be."

"Really, Chon, I would, but I promised someone I'd meet them after the show. He probably thinks I ran off with the band or something."

Chon had expected, wanted, nothing more than a greasy omelet at an all-night diner in the company of someone he had missed so much for so long, of his only friend in town. Still, the word *he* in Araceli's sentence cut him. He knew he had no right to be wounded, so he moved on. "Okay," he said. "Well, let me walk you to your car. Where are you parked?"

Araceli smiled and gave a bit of a laugh.

"Right here. Someone pulled out when I got here. I figured it was my lucky day."

Chon nodded. "Was it?"

"It was a good one," she said. "I'll call you. I promise. We'll catch up."

Chon nodded.

She pulled him in for a tight hug and gave him a slow, tender kiss on the cheek. Her lips still on his face, Chon regretted again not moving to kiss her. Nothing would have been regained. In fact, he may well have lost what ground he'd made back up that night in reconnecting with a friend. Just trying—trying and being rejected or trying and connecting and reopening old wounds more than they already were—would have been worth it.

Chon wasn't done loving Araceli. As she got in her car and pulled away, not waiting until she was out of sight to call the *he* she was driving towards, Chon knew he would never be done loving her.

Walking to his own car, not even thinking of joining his friends on Sixth, Chon understood that Araceli's love had shaped him, made him who he was and how he would love for the rest of his life. Every woman he would ever meet would be measured against Araceli. Even when he was done missing her outright, when he would come to forget the things they talked about and the movies they saw together, she would be the standard by which he loved. He would remember to love better than he loved her, to be better than he was with her, to her. She was the foundation for how he would treat the world, and so of who he was.

Years from then, after loves gained and lost, after years of marriage, one of his kids will find a picture of Chon and Araceli holding hands, kissing—a picture Chon had long since shown his wife and forgotten he had—and will feel a cold jolt of panic: could there ever have been a reality in which they did not exist, in which Mom and Dad didn't exist, in which their father was happy with another woman—a beautiful woman?

The panic will be so real and tactile that Chon's kid will hold off asking him about it until he grows old and gray and forgetful. Chon will smile when he sees the photo. Araceli will no longer be a person in a picture, or even that old picture, so real and true a representation of a moment in time, in that old box of useless souvenirs. She will be the dust that covers the glass in the frame, the Vaseline on the lens separating the now from the then, giving it a patina of nostalgia and all the hopes and fears the past held for the present.

If he forgot everything—his past, his childrens' faces, his name, though he will still have the sounds of his breath and his heart beating steady inside his chest—she will have affected every part of who he was.

When he is done considering the picture his son or daughter holds before him, he will tell them a story about a beautiful girl and teenage boy who was filled with lust. They are only bit players in a larger tale about leaving home and falling in love and growing up to learn from so many mistakes and embarrassing insecurities. He will tell them the story of how he became who he is, and that story will begin with two boys named John leaving town on a trip that was destined to end with them dying.

ACKNOWLEDGMENTS

Thank you Wag-a-Bag and La Jolla Village Mobil.
Thank you Hebbronville and Corpus Christi.
Thank you Uncle Mike and Austin.
Thank you Moody.
Thank you Ulyana.

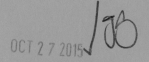